CAEL

WERE ZOO BOOK ELEVEN

R. E. BUTLER

Cael

Were Zoo Book Eleven

By R. E. Butler

CAEL (WERE ZOO BOOK ELEVEN)
BY R. E. BUTLER

Cover by CT Cover Creations

This ebook is a work of fiction. Names, characters, places, and incidents are the product of the author's imagination and not to be construed as real. Any resemblance to actual persons, living or dead, events or locations is coincidental.

Disclaimer: The material in this book is for mature audiences only and contains graphic sexual content and is intended for those older than the age of 18 only.

Edited by Sarah Dawn Johnson

Thanks to Joyce, Shelley, and Ann for beta reading.

CAEL (WERE ZOO BOOK ELEVEN)
BY R. E. BUTLER

November Jones is the product of a one-night stand. She didn't know her father except to curse his name and the weird genetics he left her with. She wouldn't give him a single thought if it weren't for the fact that he tried to kill her several times and she and her mother have been on the run since she was a toddler. When an invitation for a safari tour shows up in the mail addressed to the previous occupant, Novi feels compelled to go.

Elephant shifter Cael spends his days as the in-house veterinarian at the Amazing Adventures Safari Park taking care of the normal animals and his nights underground with the other shifters, staying hidden from humans. It's a day like any other when he's in his shift in the paddock while the safari tour vehicles drive by…until he smells something amazing and knows the beautiful brunette VIP is his soulmate.

The problem? Novi is no ordinary human. Can Cael and the shifters in the park keep Novi and her mom safe in the park or will Novi's father finally catch up to them?

CHAPTER ONE

Cael Donnelly shoved his feet into his work boots and laced them, then stood and picked up the gift bag from the coffee table. His friend and fellow elephant shifter, Kelley, had just had a baby with his soulmate, Rhapsody. The little one was one week old, and Cael hadn't seen the baby since he'd been brought home the day he was born. The couple hadn't wanted to know the sex of the baby in advance, so Cael had decided to wait to get them a gift.

He'd had to call his mom and ask her what was appropriate, because he'd had no idea what to get for them. With her advice, he'd settled on something called a onesie with cartoon elephants on it and an infant rattle shaped like a black cat, since Rhapsody was a black panther shifter.

Leaving his house, which was in the elephants' private living quarters underneath the Amazing Adventures Safari Park in New Jersey, he headed to Kelley and Rhapsody's home. He knocked on the front door and heard Kelley's muffled "Come in."

"Hey," he said when he opened the front door and found the trio sitting on the couch in the family room.

"Hey yourself," Rhapsody said, lifting little Khap onto her shoulder and patting his back. "It's so nice of you to stop by."

"I would've dropped this off sooner, but I was afraid to wake the baby," Cael said. He handed the gift to Kelley and sat in a comfortable chair across from them.

"He's a great sleeper so far," Rhapsody said. "We're very lucky."

"And also hoping it stays that way," Kelley said.

Kelley took Khap from his mate and gave her the gift. Rhapsody pulled out the blue and green tissue paper from inside the bag and took out the onesie and rattle. "Oh! You got something for each of our animals, that's so cool! Thank you!"

She beamed at Cael, and he made a mental note to thank his mom for the advice. "You're welcome."

"Wanna hold him?" Kelley asked.

Before Cael could answer one way or the other, Kelley set the little boy in Cael's arms. Khap smelled like powder and the mixture of both animals—the dry sweetness of savannah grass and the deep earthiness of the jungle. Cael's heart clenched as he looked down at the baby, smiling as he stretched his little arms and yawned.

"He's a good-looking kid," Cael said with a low voice.

"Takes after his daddy," Rhapsody said.

Cael was a little jealous. Well, a whole hell of a lot jealous, because Kelley was the only elephant in the memory who'd found his soulmate. Rhapsody had bought a ticket for the VIP safari tour, which had been arranged by the alphas to draw in unmated male and female humans to the park. The hope had been that their people would find soulmates among the humans, but while the tours had been running for a long time, few soulmates had actually come from the tours themselves.

Looking down at this little baby, so sweet and cute, made

him long for that in his own life. He could do what his mother wanted him to—which she herself had done—and find an elephant to mate with solely to have a child and not for a life-long mating. His mother and father were not mated, but neither had ever mated others. While both his parents believed he should've had a child years earlier and not waited, they weren't romantics at heart like Cael was. He wanted to wait for his soulmate. He didn't want to mate with a random female simply to have a child, he wanted to build a life with the one female on the planet meant for him, and in order to do that he had to wait for her.

He'd certainly like it if she hurried up, though. His bed was damn lonely.

"You look like you're thinking about something," Kelley said.

Cael looked up and realized that Rhapsody was gone. Kelley explained she went to take a shower while Khap was sleeping.

"I was thinking about my soulmate."

"You'll find her when the time is right."

"Everyone always says that."

"Well, it's true. You don't want to go into an arranged mating or have a child without finding your soulmate, so you have no choice but to wait. Once you find her, though, your whole world is going to change in a heartbeat. Finding Rhapsody was like suddenly realizing that part of me had been missing and I hadn't ever realized it. She completes me."

Cael rolled his eyes. "You're getting really poetic there, bro."

"Love will do that to a male. Wait and see how goofy you sound when you find your soulmate."

Cael and Kelley talked for a while longer, with Cael holding his friend's son and thinking about how much he longed for what Kelley had. He knew it would be his someday, he just hoped he'd find his soulmate sooner rather than later.

Cael's phone buzzed, alerting him that his shift was about to start. He handed the still-sleeping Khap over to his father. "Where did you guys get his name, anyway? It's cool."

"It's our names together. Rhapsody was trying to combine my first and middle names to come up with a new name, and I suggested we use both our first names and see what we could come up with. As soon as we said Khap, we both loved it."

"Maybe you'll start a trend in the park of combining names."

"I think because Khap is unique as an elephant-panther hybrid that having a unique name suits him."

"You're really lucky, Kelley. Congrats."

"You'll be lucky too someday, trust me. I believe with my whole heart that every shifter has a soulmate out there somewhere, it just requires a whole lot of patience."

Cael said goodbye and left the house, shutting the door quietly so he didn't wake Khap.

"Hey."

Cael looked up and saw his alpha, Alistair, walking out of his house. There were only four elephants in the memory led by Alistair. Kelley and Cael had both come from other memories, but Indio had been part of Alistair's memory and followed him when he came to New Jersey to join with the other shifters. Cael was a veterinarian and handled the non-shifter animals, which they referred to as the "norms." Alistair, Indio, and Kelley cleaned the paddocks and tended to the norms, but Cael was solely responsible for the norms' health and welfare. He'd come to New Jersey when he was eighteen, and after spending time with the norms, he'd decided to go to college to be able to take care of them. There were three sections of norms—rhinos were in one paddock, giraffes were in another, and deer, antelope, and a cranky Moose named Tank were in a third. A bird sanctuary had been created in the fall and was run by owl shifter Jess and her wolf mate Auden, and while birds were not his specialty, he helped with the rehabbing and care of the natural birds whenever he could.

"You heading topside?" Cael asked as he caught up to his alpha.

"In a little while. I have a meeting with the alphas to discuss the VIP tour."

"What about it?"

"We're just going to look at the numbers and see if there's a way to cut costs for the tours without sacrificing what they were designed for. We probably need to either do more tours in a day or add a day."

"So long as you're not planning to stop them."

"Not even a little bit," he said. "We're also talking about whether we can get into some online advertising and encourage people to register online which would help with printing and shipping costs for the paper tickets."

"Advertising sounds like a good idea to me."

"Me too. We'll see what the number crunchers say."

"Good luck," Cael said.

"Thanks. I'll see you up in the paddocks after the meeting."

The two parted ways, his alpha heading out into the hall to go to the conference room as Cael opened the door that led to a stairwell that would take him up into the norms' paddocks. He could get topside three ways—through the main hall, with a stairwell that would take him directly to the employee cafeteria, through a stairwell that would take him into the elephant paddock, and through a second stairwell that would take him into one of the norms' paddocks. Both paddock entrances opened up in the floor of large maintenance sheds in the paddocks, so he could get into the paddock without having to walk all the way around the park.

He climbed the stairs and opened the door in the floor that led to his favorite of the norm paddocks: the one with Tank. The moose's full name was Cantankerous, and he was the park's unofficial mascot. Cael was going to check each deer and antelope to ensure they were healthy, give them their vitamins, and set out feed, and then he'd see if Tank would cooperate with an exam. Sometimes the moose would, and sometimes he'd try to swing his big antlers around like he wanted to stab people. The norms trusted the elephant shifters so they were able to get up close with them. Predator shifters like wolves and bears couldn't even set foot in the norm paddocks without causing problems. The only predator shifter who could be in the norm paddocks without issue was Rhapsody, and they were fairly certain it was because she and Kelley were mated and the norms sensed she wasn't a threat.

After gathering his supplies, he headed out of the maintenance shed and stopped, looking around the huge paddock. He took in a deep breath of spring morning air and tried to clear his head of everything but the tasks at hand, but no matter how he tried to focus on his work alone, he couldn't shake the thoughts of finding his soulmate.

Hurry up and come to me. I promise to wait for you.

He hoped she would somehow hear his silent plea and come to the park so their paths would cross. He couldn't wait for the next chapter of his life to begin.

CHAPTER TWO

Novi Jones checked her watch as she strolled into the storage room of the Nifty Thrifty Thrift Store to check out the boxes donated from a local library. She was a bookworm of the highest order and particularly loved old books. Working at a thrift store often gave her the opportunity to look for unique books among donations. That she had four boxes to go through from the library was a boon. She hoped she'd find some good romances for herself and some cookbooks for her mom.

"I'm going to take a break, Novi," the store manager, Katya, said. Her eyes went wide as she looked at the stack of four boxes that was taller than Novi. "Holy crap, let me help you."

Together they lifted the boxes one by one and set them on the floor. "Thanks," Novi said. "I'll keep an eye on the front in case anyone comes inside."

Katya nodded. "I have to make a couple phone calls and I never took my break earlier. Holler if you need me."

Novi nodded and turned her attention to one box, keeping her ears attuned for the telltale ring of the bell signaling someone had come into the store. The first box was full of DVDs, so Novi closed the lid and pushed the box to the section of the storage room for electronic-related items to be shelved. The second box held a mishmash of non-fiction, from war stories to gardening to biographies.

She sat back on her heels and took out one of the books titled "Grow Your Own Food," with pictures of fruits and vegetables on the front. Novi actually enjoyed gardening, but she and her mom moved too frequently to really get a garden going.

Her thoughts turned bitter for a moment. Why the hell did they have to live in hiding and move every six months, or whenever her mom felt like they were being watched? Little girls often dreamed of growing up to be a princess or an astronaut or finding Prince Charming, but all Novi had ever dreamed of was staying in one place long enough to make friends. Maybe she could have attended a real school instead of being homeschooled.

Shoving the dark thoughts away, she set the gardening book to the side and decided to see if she could start some kind of container garden they could take with them when they moved again. Or, maybe, she could convince her mom to stick around. So far, Novi liked New Jersey. The small town of Little Neck—which she supposed was named after the type of clams—was quaint and friendly, and the spacious yard of their rental home backed up to a forest refuge so she had loads of acreage to roam in. She adored being out in the woods in nature. Her mom said she was born wearing hiking boots.

The front bell rang, and Novi stood and dusted off her jeans before heading out to greet the customers.

"I'm looking for a wedding dress," the young woman who appeared to be in her early twenties said. A woman who looked like a slightly older version of her was staring at the row of wedding gowns along the wall with a scowl.

"All of our gowns are on that wall," Novi said, pointing to where they were both looking.

They walked to the wall and quickly flipped through them. Novi had really good hearing, so she heard them making comments about the low quality of gowns available. Novi mentally rolled her eyes. It never failed to surprise her when people expected top quality items at thrift stores. Sometimes—rarely—something amazing came into the store, like a priceless painting or real jewelry or a couture dress, but those times were few and far between.

"I want to see what you have in the back," the older woman announced, turning to look at Novi.

"What we have is out already," Novi said.

"I don't believe you," she said with a sniff. "I want you to go look in the back and bring out any dresses you find."

Novi had the urge to growl and bare her teeth at the irritating woman, but she tamped down the feeling. "I assure you that there are no wedding gowns in the back."

"You're lying," the young woman said.

Novi's gums ached suddenly, and she ground her teeth together to stop the ache before she spoke. "I beg your pardon?"

"A friend of a friend said she read on social media that a wedding store had donated a bunch of gowns to this thrift store and they were being held back for some kind of promotional sales push. We want to see them now."

Novi inhaled and exhaled slowly. "That's simply not true. We haven't gotten a shipment from anyone with wedding dresses and we don't do promos like you're suggesting. Your information isn't accurate, so perhaps you have the wrong store. I'll say it again, what we have is what you see, period."

"Get your manager, right this instant!" the older woman said, her tone furious.

Novi's fingers tingled, and she clenched them together as she turned to get Katya from the office. Novi had no idea why she was feeling so emotional, but it sometimes happened. Her mom said they were panic attacks from being confronted, but Novi didn't feel panicked, just pissed. The women had no right to question her integrity off some random social media post. It was a thrift store for goodness sake.

She quickly explained the situation to Katya.

"Wow," Katya said. She rose to her feet and then froze, staring intently at Novi's face.

"What?" Novi asked.

"Your eyes are blue. I thought...aren't they usually brown?"

Novi blinked rapidly a few times and tried to calm down. "They change color when I get emotional. Those women pissed me off."

"Ah, my eyes get really green when I cry. I've never heard of eyes changing color completely, but that's pretty cool. Well, it's not cool you were treated badly. I'll handle them, you hang out back here and take a break."

"Thanks. I really need one."

Novi went to the tiny bathroom and flicked on the overhead light. Sure enough, her chocolate brown eyes were an icy-blue color with gold striations.

She rubbed the space over her heart with her fingertips. Her skin tingled and the urge to growl rose again.

She'd had these strange symptoms when she was overly emotional—eyes changing color, gums and fingers tingling, and wanting to growl or snarl. She'd had them for years, even since she could remember. The first time she ever actually growled at someone was when she was in public school in kindergarten and a little girl had taken her fingerpaints. That was the one and only day she'd been in public school. Her mom had snatched her out of there really fast.

Panic attack? It just felt like something inside her wanted justice in a feral sort of way. To lash out with claws and bare fangs she didn't have.

It sure didn't feel like a panic attack.

She knew she couldn't tell her mom about the incident, because her mom would freak out and tell her to quit the job she'd only had for a week. And she might get scared enough to move them again when they'd only been in New Jersey for a few weeks. She'd keep the situation to herself. She could handle it, she just had to remember to walk away before she did anything strange in front of people.

If only she could figure out why she felt like she did and had these weird episodes. She was certain it was related to her biological father, but that bastard was never going to give her any information. He was the reason they were on the run in the first place.

He'd tried to kill her when she was a toddler.

"Wow, those women were bitches!" Katya said, walking into the storage room.

Novi chuckled. "Yeah. What did you say to them?"

"I told them if they wanted dresses from a wedding shop they needed to go to one and not expect miracles at a thrift shop. And that if they didn't like our selection they could kindly shove it up their ass."

"You didn't!"

"Well, I was diplomatic. They're gone, and they'll probably post on social media that this is a terrible place to shop, but who the hell cares? We have a great clientele who come in looking for deals and are nice to boot, we don't need bitches calling us liars. Which, PS, is like the opposite way to get me to want to help someone out."

"Yeah, me too. Thanks for handling it."

"That's what I'm here for."

Katya returned to the office, and Novi knelt in front of the boxes and poked around, moving books from one box to the other and setting aside ones that caught her eye. By the time the store was closed at eight and her shift was over a half hour later, she'd found two air fryer cookbooks for her mom, and two old romances with swashbuckling pirates on the front covers for herself, the heroes both with open shirts and long flowing hair just like the ladies in their arms. She'd also found a container garden book, which she thought would be fun to look into.

She paid for the books and placed them in her knapsack, then said goodnight to her boss.

The car she shared with her mom had seen better days, but it worked, as did the radio, and that was enough for her. The drive across town took only seven minutes. The house she shared with her mom was a cute three-bedroom ranch with a red front door and a small porch. They were on a quiet street with the houses spread far apart, which was what her mom looked for when house hunting. They generally stayed away from apartment complexes because they were too close together and could lead to people asking too many questions.

Once more she thought about how unfair the situation was. She wanted to stay put and make friends and build a life. They hadn't heard from her father in several years, but her mom was still worried about being found.

She parked in the gravel driveway and went to get the mail. Inside the box was a few pieces of junk mail and something from the Amazing Adventures Safari Park, addressed to the previous tenant.

Novi turned the large, colorful postcard from the park over and read it as she walked up the drive to the house. The postcard was actually a ticket for a free VIP safari tour and doubled as a parking pass. While it was addressed to the previous tenant, it didn't say anywhere on the ticket that it was non-transferrable. She decided to check out the website and see if she could make a reservation for a tour. She'd never been to the park and going on a private safari tour sounded really fun.

Opening the front door, she called out for her mom and found her in the kitchen dunking chocolate chip cookies in a glass of milk. Novi kissed her cheek and set the mail down on the worn table.

"How was work?" her mom, Lori, asked.

"Good." She skipped the part about the rude women and her reaction to them and instead opened her knapsack and took out the cookbooks.

"Oh, fun! I'll find something new to try this weekend."

"I'm sure it will be delicious."

"What's this?" her mom asked as Novi reached for the ticket to put it in her pack.

"It came in the mail."

"Well, it's trash. Toss it with the other stuff."

"I think I'll go on the tour. It's free."

"It's not addressed to you."

"I was going to see if I could use the ticket even if it's not addressed to me."

Her mom narrowed her eyes. "Um, no. We don't do that kind of thing."

"What, go to the zoo?"

"Yes. They take pictures in public places like that and post them online. It would be just our bad luck for your father to see your picture somewhere and know where we are. So put the thought from your mind. If you want to see animals, go for a walk in the woods."

"Mom, I think you're overreacting. It's been a long time."

"Need I remind you that the last time he found out where we lived, he almost ran me off the road and killed us both? He's unstable and unstoppable. Trust me to take care of us and keep us both safe." She took the ticket and tossed it into the trash with the junk mail.

Novi wanted to protest, but she could see the firm set of her mom's jaw and knew it was futile. She'd come back for the ticket after her mom went to bed. If she didn't want Novi to go on a tour, then she'd just do it on her own. She was twenty-two and could make decisions for herself. There was no harm in going to the zoo, she was sure of it.

But more than that, she had a feeling... like it was kismet and she was destined to find that ticket and go on the tour. She wasn't about to mess with destiny, so she was going to go to the park, no matter what.

CHAPTER THREE

Novi didn't like deception in any form. She particularly didn't like lying to her mom about anything. But she couldn't shake the feeling that she needed to go to the park and go on the tour. After her mom went to bed Thursday night, Novi used the laptop to search up the safari park and found a link to the tours. She entered the information from the ticket and reserved a tour for Saturday afternoon. The next day, she told Katya she'd have to take off early Saturday for an appointment.

Novi put a change of clothes and a toiletries bag in her knapsack Saturday morning and said goodbye to her mom, then headed to the thrift store. The day eeked by, and she was certain it was because she was so excited about the tour. By the time she could clock out, she thought it had been the longest day on record. She changed into a pair of jeans, a navy-blue t-shirt, and a light-weight olive green jacket. After switching out her sturdy work shoes for her favorite tennis shoes, she ran a brush through her long, dark brown hair, put on some makeup, and gave herself one last look in the small mirror over the sink.

"You look great," Katya said when Novi walked into the main part of the store.

"Thanks. I'll see you on Monday!"

"Have fun."

Novi put her knapsack on the floor of the backseat and took out her wristlet wallet and the tour ticket. She plugged the park address into the map app on her phone and then put on her favorite radio station.

After thirty minutes, she'd arrived at the park. It was a beautiful April day, and she wasn't surprised the park was packed. There was a line all the way to the road to get into the park, and she was glad she'd left earlier than necessary so she wasn't late.

Once she got up to the parking lot attendant, she showed him the ticket and he said, "Welcome to the park! Follow the signs for the VIP tour lot. Have fun!"

"Thank you."

She parked and walked through large iron gates, weaving through the crowd to get to one of the ticket takers. "Do you have ID?" the young man asked as he took her ticket and looked at it.

"I do," she said, taking her license from her wristlet. "But my name's not on that ticket."

"Oh? Where did you get the ticket from?" He looked from her ID to the ticket and then at her.

She explained how she came to have the ticket. "I did make a reservation for a tour, but if I can't use this ticket maybe I can just pay for a tour myself?"

"Oh no, that's not necessary," he said, handing the ID and ticket back to her. "The tickets are transferrable, and clearly we had a bad address for this person, so it's nice that the ticket is being used. Just let them know at the check-in for the tour what you told me, and there shouldn't be any problem."

"Thanks," she said.

"Enjoy the tour."

He gave her a map, showing her where the tour was located. She followed the crowd into the park and turned left toward the tour. The three men at the tour check-in let her through without issue. As she took her place in line, she blew out a breath of relief, thankful she hadn't been told she couldn't use someone else's ticket.

There was one young woman in line ahead of her, snapping her gum and taking selfies. Novi leaned back to avoid being caught in the background of her numerous photos, thankful when a blue camo-colored Jeep pulled forward and called for the woman to go on her tour. Novi was all alone in line. She could hear the Jeep as it moved away, the rustle of the trees around her in the gentle spring breeze, and felt the heat of the sun as it streamed through the branches overhead.

"Are you Novi?" a man asked quietly, startling her out of her reverie.

She gasped and pressed her hand to her chest like a lady in a romance novel. "Yes, sorry."

"I'm Benjamin, your tour guide. Would you like something to drink?"

"No thanks, I'm good."

She followed Benjamin to the Jeep and climbed into the back seat next to a black bag that he explained held a professional camera. "We'll take your picture at each paddock, and then you'll be given a souvenir photo album after the tour is over, free of charge."

"That's pretty neat."

The driver looked over his shoulder at her and smiled. "I'm Silvanus. Have you been on a tour before?"

"Not like this. I just moved to New Jersey a few weeks ago with my mom. It's my first time at the park."

"Then we'll make sure you have a great time," Silvanus said. "Hold on, the Jeep lurches a bit when it takes off."

Benjamin spoke into a walkie as they pulled up to a gate. A moment later, the gate squeaked as it opened, and the Jeep moved through the opening and followed a path.

"Do you have a favorite animal?" Benjamin asked as the Jeep jostled along the dirt path.

"I kind of just like all animals, but I've always thought wolves were pretty cool."

"Us too," Benjamin said with a grin. "First up are the elephants. We've got four male elephants in the memory."

"Elephant groups are called memories? That's funny."

"Lots of animal groups have weird names, like gorillas are a band and cheetahs are a coalition," Silvanus said.

"I learned the other day that a group of bats is called a cauldron, which is super fitting, I think," Benjamin said with a chuckle.

The Jeep pulled to a stop, and Benjamin helped Novi down and then grabbed the camera from the bag. She turned toward the high chain-link fence and saw four elephants milling around the paddock.

Her heart started to pound as she walked toward the fence, and her gums and fingers ached suddenly. She glanced down at her fingers and saw that the pale pink polish didn't quite cover the fact that her nails had darkened.

Shit.

Why was she having this weird emotional reaction right now? She wasn't upset or angry, so what was causing it?

There was a snuffling sound, and she jerked her head up to see a huge elephant staring down at her.

She grasped the links and curled her fingers over the cool metal. The elephant touched her fingers with his trunk and awareness shot up her arm like electricity. It was as if she actually knew this elephant, recognized him even though she'd never seen an elephant in person in her life.

Turning her hand over, she rubbed the warm skin of his trunk, marveling at how close he was. How big he was.

"Hey. Whoa," Benjamin said. "We don't really recommend touching the animals, Novi."

The elephant snorted and tossed his head, his ears flapping with the motion.

Benjamin looked up at him and said, "Ah, I get it. Hey Novi, why don't you turn around and I'll take a pic of you with the elephant."

"Does he have a name?" she asked, slipping her fingers away from the fence and turning to face Benjamin.

"Um, yeah, but I don't remember what it is off the top of my head."

"Oh. He's really big."

Benjamin chuckled and tried to cover it with a cough. He told her to smile and she did, giggling when the elephant touched her shoulder through the fence. She turned back around and said, "I wish I could stay. You're pretty neat. I also wish I knew your name. Maybe someone else will know it."

The something in her chest that wanted to growl when she was upset stuttered to life like a purr, and this time she didn't try to stop it. Benjamin was already walking away, and it was just her and the elephant. It wasn't like he'd know there was something wrong with her because she could growl. He touched her fingers again and made a soft rumbling sound, and her growl grew louder until she had to take a step back because her eyes were stinging with tears.

"Wow, I'm feeling so emotional right now I can't even figure out why. I should go." She shook her head at herself. "I have no idea why I'm talking to you like you're a person. I must be crazy. Or hungry. Or tired. Or all three." She looked up, up, up at him and smiled. "Bye."

As she walked toward the Jeep, the elephant lifted his trunk and trumpeted loudly, and she felt the sound all the way to the center of her being. It sounded possessive and protective...of her.

With a last look at him, she waved as the Jeep pulled away, not turning around until she couldn't see him any longer.

"Do they always come up to the fence like that?" she asked.

"Nope, you must be special," Silvanus said.

Her cheeks heated, and she smiled. "That's a nice thought, but I'm just a regular girl."

"Maybe," Benjamin said. "Or maybe you have a special connection to animals and he was just reacting to it. Where are you from, anyway?"

"All over. We move a lot."

"For work?" Silvanus asked.

It was easier to lie than to tell the truth to strangers, even though she hated lying. "Yeah. My mom and I don't stay in one place too long."

"It's just the two of you?" Benjamin asked.

"Yeah. My father didn't want to be part of our lives."

Or, she told herself, *he didn't want her to be alive in the first place*. But that was a truth she'd never shared with anyone and wasn't about to spill her guts to two strangers on a safari tour.

They continued on the tour, visiting the wolves, then the gorillas, and then the bears. When she got out of the Jeep at the bear paddock, she felt another twinge of familiarity with the bears, but she pushed away the thoughts and focused on the tour guide who told her some interesting facts about the various types of bears in the paddock. She kept her distance, not wanting to have another growling episode, and was relieved to get back into the Jeep and on their way to the other paddocks. She'd been looking forward to seeing Tank the grumpy moose, and he didn't disappoint. He was really a beautiful animal with his huge horns and dark fur.

When they reached the end of the tour, Benjamin said, "I'm going to take you to the office so you can wait for your photo album. It shouldn't take too long."

"Okay, thank you. It was fun."

"I'm glad you enjoyed it," Benjamin said.

She said goodbye to Silvanus and walked with Benjamin to the security office.

"Have you been a tour guide long?" she asked.

"A couple years. What do you do?"

"I work at a thrift store."

"You must see some neat old things."

"From time to time. It would be fun to work with animals, though."

"It is."

They stopped at a small building with a sign over the door that designated it as the security office. Benjamin opened the door for her, and she thanked him for escorting her and being a great guide.

"It was nice to meet you, Novi. Have a great afternoon."

"Thanks, Benjamin, you too." She stepped inside the building and the door shut behind her.

A tall man with dark hair stood behind a long counter.

"You must be Novi," he said with a smile.

"I am. How did you know my name?"

"Benjamin radioed that he was bringing you here for your album. It's being loaded and then printed. It's going to take about an hour. I'm Xavier."

"Nice to meet you. Do I have to stay here the whole time? I'm kind of hungry."

21

"Actually, since they're a little backed up at the print shop, the tour's sending someone to take you on a private tour of the whole park which includes a free meal. If you like burgers, there's a stall in the park that has the best ones."

"That sounds perfect."

"Good. It won't be long, Cael's on his way."

She sat in one of the chairs along a bank of windows and took out her phone, realizing she'd missed a text from her mom asking how her day was going. She replied that she was having a great day and then she put her phone up, her mind a jumble as she thought about the elephant on the tour.

She wondered if Cael would think it was crazy if she asked to go see him one more time.

CHAPTER FOUR

Cael headed to the elephant paddock from the private living space, coming up the stairs into the mainte-nance shed. He found Alistair waiting in the shed, with Kelley and Indio already out and milling around in their shifts. Rhapsody was playing the part of zookeeper, wearing a beige uniform and cleaning the paddock alongside her mate. Because Rhapsody was a black panther and the park had no black panther paddock, she didn't shift for the public tours, but shifted after hours to run around with Kelley.

Cael dropped the hinged lid to close the stairs with a sigh.

"Something wrong?" Alistair asked, looking up from his phone.

"My elephant's been driving me crazy all day."

"Crazy how?" Alistair put his phone on the workbench and folded his arms over his chest.

"I don't know, just noisy. Anxious. I can't figure out why, but it's making me bonkers."

"They can be a pain in the ass sometimes," he said with a chuckle. "Hopefully shifting will help."

"I hope so."

As it was, his elephant was urging him to shift and get out into the paddock. He wished he could actually talk to his elephant and get a real response, but all he ever got was feelings and urges. Alistair stripped and shifted, leaving the maintenance shed which had a door large enough for them to walk through in their shifts. Cael followed suit and ducked out of the shed, turning to close the doors with his trunk. He shook himself out fully, from his huge ears to his tail and then stretched. It was a beautiful day and he was with his closest friends, but despite shifting and the beauty surrounding him, his beast was still anxious.

Letting out a sigh, he lumbered over to Rhapsody who was sitting on a hay bale and tossing apples in the air for Kelley to catch.

Cael realized that little Khap was in a sling against her chest, his head tilted to the side as he slumbered.

Rhapsody tossed an apple at Cael, and he caught it and ate it quickly.

Cael roamed the paddock, his elephant's anxiety not ebbing in any way.

He heard the tell-tale rumble of a Jeep which signaled the VIP tours had started. There were four vehicles, each carrying a driver and guide with room for the VIP. The guide told facts about each animal group at the paddocks, but the point of the tours was not about the animals, but about finding soulmates. At this point, after dozens of weekends with hours in their shifts, only five soulmates had come from the tours—two for gorillas, one for a bear, one for a lion, and one for an elephant. Cael was happy for the males who had found their soulmates through the tours, but he knew that everyone was disappointed that more soulmates hadn't been found. It seemed like a simple enough idea—bring in unmated human males and females and hope for soulmate matches, it just wasn't as effective in reality as they'd all hoped it would be.

He joined his friends near the fence, watching as Jeeps stopped and a human male or female climbed out, walked to the fence for a pic, and then got back in the Jeep. With each human, the tour guide would wait to see if one of the elephants felt a connection and when they didn't, the Jeep would head to the next paddock.

As Jeep after Jeep stopped and then moved on, Cael grew disheartened. But his elephant was still anxious and...excited?

He mulled over the feelings as another Jeep pulled to a stop in front of the paddock.

A light breeze blew in his direction, and he caught the most delicious scent—the female in the Jeep.

She smelled amazing...like honey and sunshine.

His beast went nuts in his head, trumpeting loudly and making him feel like he'd go deaf from the inside out. He marched to the fence and inhaled again, but this time he picked up something more as she climbed from the Jeep and walked to the fence.

She smelled like a shifter.

Bear if he wasn't mistaken, but not the grizzly and black bears in the park. He wasn't sure what type of bear she smelled like, and the scent was subtle and not as strong as other shifters.

His curiosity was overridden by his elephant's excitement as she curled her fingers over the fence. He touched her fingers with his trunk and awareness jolted through him. She was his soulmate.

And she was stunning.

Curved for days, beautiful dark brown eyes...no wait, they were pale blue? What the hell was going on?

"Hey, whoa," Benjamin said. "We don't really recommend touching the animals, Novi."

Cael tossed his head back with an annoyed grunt, and Benjamin clearly understood that something more was going on than with the usual VIP tour. "Ah, I get it," the wolf male said with a nod. "Hey, Novi, why don't you turn around and I'll take a pic of you with the elephant."

"Does he have a name?" she asked, slipping her fingers away from the fence, turning for the picture.

"Um, yeah, but I don't remember what it is off the top of my head."

Cael mentally rolled his eyes. The tour guides used to tell guests what their names were, but the last time someone went on the tour and found their soulmate, she'd been told the gorilla's name and then thought someone was playing a prank on her when she met the actual male with the same name. Now they didn't tell people the shifters' names, only the normal, non-shifting animals.

"Oh. He's really big."

Benjamin chuckled and tried to cover it with a cough. Cael touched her shoulder through the fence, not wanting to lose the connection. She turned to face him and declared she wished she could stay longer, and he was of the same mind. Unfortunately, she had to leave for the rest of the tour.

She let out a soft growl and rubbed her fingers against his trunk and then stepped away. Her eyes were glistening with tears.

He watched her leave, desperately wanting to rip the fence apart and follow, but he knew he couldn't. He did the only thing he could at the moment and that was lift his trunk high in the air and trumpet loudly. The sound blasted from him, full of joy at finding the other half of his heart.

His friends joined in.

Once the Jeep was gone, Cael turned and hurried to the shed to shift so he could meet his soulmate at the office. He changed back to human and dressed, then opened the door and found Alistair standing just outside.

"She's my soulmate," he said excitedly.

Alistair nodded, his ears flapping.

"I think she's a shifter. Bear, maybe. But her scent is weird, it's kind of watered down or not strong. I'm not sure what it means."

Rhapsody walked up, snacking on one of the apples. "What would it mean if her scent is not strong? I thought you either smelled like a shifter or you smelled human."

He looked at her baby. "Khap smells like you and Kelley. Maybe my soulmate is a mix and I just can't pick up what the other shifter type is."

"You'd think she would've said something to let you know she knew you're a shifter," she mused.

He shrugged. "Maybe she didn't trust the people with her."

"Maybe. Well, go see her! I can't wait to meet her. I hope you're able to bring her to meet everyone soon."

"Me too. But I have to follow protocol and that means I can't tell her what I am, she has to tell me she knows."

"Good luck!"

Cael smiled and pulled the shed door shut, then hurried down the stairs. He came back up into the park through the employee cafeteria. As he hurried to the park office, he thought about what he'd seen with his soulmate. She definitely growled, but he'd also seen her nails get dark and what looked like small, pointed fangs when she opened her mouth.

And then there were her eyes, which had been brown but turned blue.

She had to be a shifter, but there was definitely something strange going on with her.

He'd have to play it cool and get to the bottom of things

fast. He didn't want to waste a minute of time in getting to know her.

"Was she why you were so excited?" he mentally asked his elephant. "Did you sense her when she came into the park?"

A happy trumpet was the answer.

He couldn't believe his beast was so in tune with their soulmate that he'd sensed her like that. No wonder he'd been feeling so anxious.

Fate had just given him the greatest gift in the world.

He reached the office and saw his soulmate sitting at the row of chairs by the windows. He took a moment to calm himself, not wanting to rush inside the building like an idiot. The last thing he wanted to do was come on too strongly.

When he felt passably normal, he opened the door to the office and walked in. He nodded to Xavier behind the counter and turned to face his female.

Damn she was gorgeous.

His tongue felt like it was glued to the roof of his mouth.

Clearing his throat, he smiled at her. "I'm Cael. You must be the VIP guest."

She rose to her feet and smiled at him, and it made his heart thud in his chest. "Hi, I'm Novi."

Their hands clasped in greeting, and he nearly fell to the floor with the power of the touch. He'd felt a jolt in his shift when he touched her fingers, but this full contact was almost too much for his system. His elephant was stomping happily in his mind.

Gathering his wits quickly, he said, "It's nice to meet you. I heard the photo albums are backed up a bit, so I came to take you on a private tour of the park."

Xavier cleared his throat. "I told her that she was also getting a free meal because of the wait."

"Of course," Cael said. They had a script they followed when a soulmate was found to give the illusion that the park was providing a service like the tour and meal to make up for the wait for the album. In reality, there was no wait for the album—they were put together really quickly. But it was important for the shifters to spend time with their soulmate and make a connection, and hopefully be able to see them again.

Cael opened the door for her and followed her out into the park. As he took her on a tour, leading with the bird sanctuary run by Auden and his mate, Jess, he asked Novi questions, trying to gently prod her to reveal information about herself. He didn't expect her to come right out and say she was a shifter, but he hoped she'd tell him something that would open up the conversation further.

By the time they made their way to the burger stall for dinner, he found Novi to be super sweet and nice, with a penchant for funny quips and occasional hilarious sarcastic comments. He and his elephant were one hundred percent smitten with her.

They sat down at a nearby picnic table with their baskets of burgers and fries. "I'm sorry you've had to move around a lot, that must be hard," he said.

"Yeah."

"Can I ask why you moved so much?"

She peered at him as she took a bite of the day's special burger—BBQ bacon and cheese—and chewed slowly. She averted her eyes.

"I'm sorry if I'm prying," he said. "I've only lived two places my whole life—Indiana with my parents and here. You seemed sad when you talked about moving so much."

She took a long drink of soda and put the cup down. "I don't know you. I'm not used to telling strangers too much about myself right off the bat."

He opened his mouth to tell her that she could tell him

anything, but she put her hand up and he clicked his teeth together.

"But that being said, I actually feel comfortable with you. I haven't felt that way in a really long time. Maybe...ever? It's so weird too, because I feel like I've met you already, but I don't know how that's possible." She chuckled. "I probably sound crazy."

"It doesn't sound crazy at all. You're right—we don't actually know each other, but I kind of feel like I've known you longer too."

"Yeah?"

He nodded. "So if you'd like to tell me your story, I'd be happy to listen. Mine is pretty boring, unless you count the time that I almost got gored by a bull when I was helping one of my professors on a farm."

She chuckled and then looked down at the half-eaten burger on her plate. "It's...not the greatest story, but I don't want you to feel sorry for me."

"I promise I won't."

"Okay." She blew out a breath. "So my dad tried to kill me."

CHAPTER FIVE

Novi winced at the blunt words she'd just uttered. Who the heck started a conversation like that?

Oh yeah, nice to meet you, super sexy guy who took me to dinner, by the way my dad hates me enough to try to kill me.

Cael's gray eyes went wide. "What?"

She pressed her lips together for a moment and then nodded. "I was the product of a one-night stand. My biological father didn't want anything to do with me, so my mom thought she was going to be on her own. But he showed up at the hospital after I was born and tried to take me. My mom got a restraining order against him, which was easy enough to do because he refused to get a blood test to determine paternity. She moved in with her sister and didn't see or hear from him for two years. Then one night she heard something in my bedroom and caught him breaking in. He said I was his child, and he wouldn't allow me to live. He tried to get to me, but my mom and aunt managed to get me out of the bedroom and called the police." She blew out a breath. She had no memory of the incident because she was so young, and she was always grateful for that fact. "My mom got scared after that and moved again, but my dad found her. So she went on the run and we've been in hiding ever since. He always seems to find us if we stay too long, so we move every six months or when she gets worried someone's paying too much attention to us."

Cael reached his hand across the table and covered hers. "I'm sorry you had to deal with that. It must be so scary to always be looking over your shoulder."

Her eyes stung with tears and she bit her lip to keep from letting the sadness overwhelm her. "I've never told anyone that," she whispered, her voice thick with emotion. "I don't know why I told you."

He gave her hand a gentle squeeze. "Maybe because you feel safe with me."

She nodded. It was true—she did feel safe with him, and she hadn't felt safe in a long, long time. "I hate it. I hate everything about being on the run and never being able to put down roots. I hate that my mom can't date or make friends because she's too afraid to stay put anywhere."

"How many times has he found you?"

"A handful of times. He's so determined. Once, when I was ten, he found us at a park and tried to grab me. If it weren't for the people around that intervened, he would've gotten me. She doesn't want us to talk about our personal lives at all, so I never was able to really make good friends or have a serious boyfriend." She shook her head and pulled her hand from his. "I don't want you to feel sorry for me or anything. I mean, I have a mom who's willing to give up everything to keep me safe. There isn't anything she wouldn't do for me, and I love her for that."

"My mom's the same way," he said, giving her a gentle smile. He picked up his burger, taking a bite. When he'd finished, he said, "Do you know anything about your dad aside from his trying to harm you?"

"What do you mean?"

"I mean, do you think you take after him physically?"

She stared at him for a long moment, wondering what he was getting at. For a heartbeat she wondered if he was talking about the way she'd growled like a freaking animal when she saw the elephant in the paddock, but she mentally tossed the idea away. He hadn't been there so he wouldn't know about it. Unless the tour guide heard her and told him?

"I don't really know," she said finally.

His gaze narrowed slightly, and she felt like he was trying to read her mind. But then he smiled. "How long has it been since you saw him?"

"Almost two years."

"Maybe he's finally given up?"

"It would be nice if that were the case," she said. "I've wanted to stop running for such a long time, but Mom's so afraid."

"It's totally understandable."

"Can we talk about something else?" she asked as she picked up what was left of her burger.

"Sure. Did you get to meet Tank the moose?"

"Well, I didn't get to meet him, but I did see him. He was drinking from the pond. He's really cool."

"Would you like to meet him?"

"How would I do that? Is he part of a petting zoo or something?"

"I'm the safari vet. I'd be happy to take you into the paddock to see him."

"Really? I...you could do that?"

"Sure. It's one of the perks of being the vet. If you don't have to leave right away, that is. We'd have to wait until the final tour is done." He glanced at his watch and said, "There's one more on the schedule."

"That would be neat. Do you think we could see the elephants?"

He blinked a few times. "Why?"

She finished the last bite of her burger and washed it down with the soda. "I just like them."

He didn't say anything for so long, she wondered if she'd crossed some kind of line. She was about to tell him to forget it, but then he said, "We can, but we can't go into the paddock like we can with Tank. The elephants are territorial."

"Oh, well one came right up to the fence to see me. He even touched my fingers with his trunk. It was pretty neat."

Cael grinned and stood. He gathered their trash and dumped it in a nearby canister then said, "How do you feel about ice cream?"

When they'd finished their cones—both of them had chosen the flavor of the day, which was strawberry cheesecake—they headed back toward the paddocks. He stopped by the booth where she'd checked in and told them he was going to take her on a walk by the paddocks since the last tour had returned.

"I've never done anything like this before," she said as they walked the opposite direction down the path to the paddock where Tank, deer, and antelope called home. "It's like a backstage pass."

Cael chuckled. "I'm glad you're excited. It's so normal to me since I've been around these guys for years, but it's exciting for me to get to share it with you."

He moved a shrub near the bottom of the tall fence and exposed a keypad. He entered a code, then there was a clicking sound. He put the shrub back in place and pushed the fence, which turned out to be a gate. It swung open, and he stepped inside and held the door for her. She walked through, and he shut the gate behind her.

The large paddock was covered with grass, with a pond and trees dotting the area.

"How many animals are in this paddock?" she asked.

"We've got seven white tailed deer and four antelope, plus Tank."

They walked toward the big shed, and Cael took her hand. Their fingers linked and she liked the way it felt to hold his hand, like it was such a natural thing to do. She wanted to rub up against him and smell him, run her fingers all over his skin.

And she wanted to growl too.

He handed her several carrots from a counter inside the shed and took some for himself. "Let's see if Tank's being friendly."

The moment they stepped out of the shed and Tank saw the carrots, he made a lowing grunt and lumbered toward them. "He's so big!" she said, giggling as the moose came near. She couldn't stop smiling as he got close enough to take a carrot from her, the green top of the vegetable swishing as he crunched loudly.

Cael rubbed Tank's nose and scratched between his antlers.

"I think he likes you," Cael said as Tank took another carrot and made a happy humming sound.

"Aw. This is so neat, thank you."

"You're welcome. I'm glad I could share it with you. Usually it's just me and the animals. It's nice to have someone with me."

"You don't have other vets here?"

They said goodbye to Tank and headed toward the gate. When they were back on the dirt path and Cael had locked the gate, he took her hand again and said, "I'm the only vet, but I do have three keepers that help out—Kelley, Indio, and Alistair."

"You must be really busy being the only vet."

He hummed and then said, "I am, but I love it."

They reached the beginning of the tour and the elephant paddock. She grasped the links and stared through them, searching for the elephant that had come so close. She counted three elephants, not four.

"I don't understand," she said.

"What do you mean?"

"Where's the one that came up to me?" She looked up at Cael, her fingers tightening on the links.

"Are you sure he's not one of those?" he asked, gesturing toward the three that were milling around.

"Positive," she said. She turned back to the paddock and shook her head. "What happened to him? What's going on?"

"Why?" he asked softly. He put his hand on her shoulder, and she felt a familiar jolt of awareness.

It was so damn much like when the elephant touched her.

But she must be losing her mind.

"You'll think I'm crazy," she whispered.

"I promise I won't. You can tell me anything, Novi."

"I felt connected to the elephant that came up to me. I can't really explain it, but I felt like I'd been destined to see him, and that makes me feel like I'm losing my marbles to be honest." She turned to face him. He was so sexy, so sweet. So protective in a way she'd never experienced before.

They'd only been together for a couple hours, but she never wanted their time together to end, even though she knew it had to.

"You're not going crazy," he said. "You felt a connection to the elephant, and judging by the way he acted toward you, he felt connected to you too."

"So what, he's my spirit animal?" she asked, rubbing the

space over her heart with her fingertips as she glanced into the paddock again, wondering where he was.

"Something like that," he said. He grasped the fence links and looked down at her. As she met her gaze, she swore she saw his eyes change from gray to brown for a moment, then back again. The same golden-brown color of the elephant that had touched her fingers.

"Cael?"

"Yeah?"

What was she going to ask him? If he was the elephant? That was not just losing-her-marbles crazy, that was lock-her-up certifiable.

Instead of speaking her mind, because she wasn't sure she could even articulate the weird thoughts, she cleared her throat and blinked away the sudden sting of tears, and said, "I need to get going. I didn't tell my mom I was coming here and if I'm too late, she'll worry."

Cael cleared his throat. "Of course. I'll walk you out and we can pick up your photo album on the way."

With a nod, she looked into the paddock one last time, wondering where her elephant was, and wondering just when she'd started to think of that particular elephant as hers.

By the time they reached her car, she was torn in half, wanting to stay but needing to go.

"Give me your phone," Cael said.

She unlocked it and handed it to him. He pushed a few buttons, and then his phone buzzed. "I just sent myself a text and added my information in your contacts. Text me and let me know you got home safely, okay?"

"Okay." She took her phone back and shivered when he tucked a lock of hair behind her ear. "Thanks for my photo album and dinner."

"It was my pleasure."

"And the tour."

He smiled.

She went onto her toes and brushed her lips across his. He hummed and as her fingers grazed the front of his shirt, she felt his chest vibrate and that feral something within her responded in kind, but with a low, happy growl.

"I'd like to see you again," Cael said, his voice rough.

"Me too. I work on Monday, but I'm off on Tuesday."

"Then I'll see you on Tuesday."

She took one last look into his gray eyes and got into her car. She pulled out of the parking spot and waved at him, then headed toward the exit. Realizing her tank was low, she stopped at the first gas station she came to and waited for the tank to be filled by the attendant.

Opening the photo album, she gasped as she saw the first picture of herself and the elephant. The big beast was right behind her at the fence, his trunk on her shoulder through the links.

And his eyes...they were the same gray as Cael's!

CHAPTER SIX

Cael slept like hell Saturday night. He tossed and turned, his elephant lamenting the fact that their soulmate wasn't with them.

He should've asked her to stay, but he knew she would've said no. She hadn't even told her mom she'd come to the park, and he'd been so distraught at her leaving that he hadn't asked her why. He could guess that it had something to do with their being in hiding.

And what the hell was he going to do about that anyway? He had no idea how to help her, but he knew he needed to. His soulmate should never be in fear of anything.

There was a knock on his door, and he pushed off the couch where he'd been arguing with his elephant for the last few hours and opened the door.

Alistair gave him a curious look. "In case you were wondering, I could hear you pacing."

"Sorry." Cael opened the door further to let in his alpha and rubbed the space between his eyes with his thumb. "I'm having a hard time."

"I'm sure." Alistair sat on the couch, and Cael joined him. "What do you think's going on? Do you think she's a shifter?"

"I don't think so," Cael said. "I think she might be a hybrid. She smells like a bear, but the scent is diluted. She also seemed fully weirded out by her reactions. If she was a full shifter, then she would've recognized me as her soulmate and that I'm a shifter, right?"

"It's possible," Alistair said, "but I scented her when we were in the paddock as well, and to me she smells more human than shifter. If she's some kind of bear, then it's one we're not familiar with in our park. But I don't think the type of bear would matter so much as the fact that the scent isn't strong. From what you told me about her past, and considering that her father has been after her for her entire life, it seems entirely logical that he's a shifter and is trying to put her down because she's a threat to their people."

"I don't understand how he can't see that she's not a threat to them, though. She clearly doesn't even know what her father is." Cael thought about how he'd asked her if she took after her father physically, which had been a leading question on his part to see if she'd tell him that she was a shifter, but she hadn't. It wasn't like he'd thought she'd just come right out and say that she was half human, half bear, but a part of him had wanted it to be that simple.

Then they could've spent the night together instead of him being miserable.

Which made him wonder if she was miserable too.

"Cael?"

He looked at his alpha. "Sorry, what?"

Alistair smiled knowingly. "It's understandable that you're distracted by meeting her and not being able to move forward with her in any significant way. When are you seeing her?"

"Tuesday."

"What are your plans?"

"I have no freaking clue. We texted a bit when she got home, but we didn't make any concrete arrangements."

"I think you should make arrangements for one or more of the bear shifters to meet you when you're out with her."

"Why?"

"Because if she's a type of bear shifter, even only part of her, she should recognize a commonality that may make her reactions stronger. Maybe Justus and Trina can meet you two out somewhere and it could appear as a coincidence."

"What would the point of that be?" Cael was frustrated as hell.

"To force the issue of her paternity. You said she seemed to stop herself from saying too much about her father, aside from his murderous tendencies. I think that speaks volumes about how she's feeling torn between her feelings for you as soulmates and her loyalty to her mom and their shared secret. I mean, hell, they don't even seem to understand what they're supposed to be keeping a secret."

Cael nodded. "I've been wondering if her mom knows that her father is a shifter or if she just thinks he's trying to kill Novi for some unknown reason."

"There are sects of shifters who are deeply hidden and keep their interactions with humans to a bare minimum. If her father is part of one of those groups, he may not have expected a pregnancy to result and then panicked when it happened. Or his alpha may have ordered him to kill her."

"I hate to say it, but it would've been better if he'd just brought her and her mom into their group and kept them close so they didn't have to worry about the secret."

"Good point. But he may have been punished for even being with a human, and then when she ran with Novi after he tried to take her from the hospital, it might have become a source of pride for him to track them down. Whatever the reason, they're clearly in danger, and a male so intent on tracking the two of them down after twenty-some years is not simply going to give up."

"Agreed. What should I do, Alistair?"

"What do you want to do?"

"Go get them and bring them here. Like right now."

His alpha chuckled. "Okay, let's call that plan b."

Cael blew out a breath and let his head fall back onto the couch cushion. "Get Novi to realize that she's not fully human so I can show her my shift. And then bring her and her mom to the park to stay so they can be safe." He lifted his head. "Could they stay in one of the apartments?"

The alphas had built an eight-unit apartment complex at the back of the park, accessible by two security gates—one leading outside the park and one inside. The complex had been built because there were human soulmates who needed a viable place to live where their families could come visit without them knowing there was a secret city underneath the park. The complex had been finished over the winter, and all the units were empty.

"I'll speak to the alphas once the sun is up this morning," Alistair said. He rose to his feet and stretched with a yawn. "In the meantime, you should try to get some rest so you're not such a grump when you talk to Novi. Make plans for Tuesday and get in touch with Justus and Trina, and then I'll call for you when I've had a chance to talk to them."

"I don't like keeping a secret from her," Cael said.

"Of course not. It goes against our nature to keep secrets from those we love, but you must for now. If you were to reveal your true self to her and she and her mom disappeared, it could put us all at risk."

"I know." Cael walked his alpha to the door and said goodnight.

"You found Novi, Cael. That's the difficult part."

They said goodnight and Cael shut the door. He stared at the couch and the space in front of it where he'd been pacing for what felt like hours. Alistair was right—he should try to get some rest. Otherwise he was going to keep pacing and be an exhausted mess for work. Even though he'd found his soulmate, he'd still need to be out in the paddock in his shift for the VIP tours that afternoon, and he had responsibilities to the norms as well. He climbed into bed, exhaustion plucking at him from all sides, and finally passed out, his last thoughts on Novi and what their future held.

Later that afternoon, Cael answered a text from Novi as he climbed the steps into the shed in the elephant paddock.

I'll be out of touch for a few hours when I'm out in the paddocks, he texted.

Okay, she texted back. *I'm supposed to be sorting through some clothes that were dropped off last night anyway. I'd rather talk to you though.*

Me too.

I'm so tired, I slept like crap last night.

Cael was secretly pleased that she hadn't slept well either, but he wasn't such an ass that he was going to let her know he was glad she'd been in turmoil. *Oh? Just not tired or was something on your mind?*

She sent him an eye roll emoji. *I think you know that I was thinking about you. How did you sleep?*

Like crap. He included a laughing emoji followed by a yawning one.

I'm bummed I had to work today and tomorrow, it would've been nice to see you. I'm looking forward to Tuesday.

Me too. Is there anything you want to do in particular?

Nope. You can plan what we do.

Immediately his thoughts strayed to his empty bed, but he pushed them away and texted, *I was thinking dinner and then we'll see where the night takes us.*

That sounds perfect. Gotta run, a customer just came in. Have fun with the animals, and give that elephant a kiss on his trunk for me.

I will.

He put his phone on the counter just as the door opened and an elephant made a grumbling sound. "I know, I know. I'm coming, Kelley. Give me a minute."

Kelley made an impatient sound, and Cael glanced at the clock on his phone and realized that the first tour was going to start in less than ten minutes. He'd lost track of time texting with Novi.

He stripped swiftly and shifted, ducking out of the shed and closing the door with his back leg.

The first Jeep holding a VIP guest came by a few minutes later. Cael hung back while the others stayed close to the fence, scenting each passing guest to see if one of them would be their soulmate.

Novi coming on the tour gave the unmated males and females in the park hope that the free tickets were actually working. He certainly could say with all honesty that without the ticket, he probably would've never met Novi. Now that he had her in his life, he wanted to keep her close.

Once the tours were done, Cael found Justus and Trina in the candy shop in the park, where Trina worked with her best friend, Lexy. Lexy was mated to Win, one of the gorillas.

The shop was empty, so Cael explained the situation. "Would you be willing to casually run into us somewhere Tuesday night?"

"Sure," Justus said. "You really think she's part bear?"

"She smells like it. Her eyes turned blue and her nails got dark, and she growled too."

Trina finished tying a bow on a clear bag of colorful taffy and said, "I don't think we should meet up at dinner. You need time to chat and get to know each other first. Maybe an ice cream shop?"

Cael pulled out his phone and searched for ice cream shops. "There's Calaways Parlor, that's only about ten minutes from her house."

"I've had their ice cream, it's really good," Trina said. "There's a Japanese steak house near there. That was always my favorite place to go for my birthday. It's exciting and fun to watch and gives you something to talk about, and the food is really good."

"That sounds perfect," Cael said. He opened the restaurant's website and made a reservation for two for six thirty on Tuesday night. "Let's meet for ice cream around eight."

"That works for us," Justus said.

"We're so happy you met your..." Trina's voice trailed off as several patrons walked into the shop. "Special someone," she said with a low voice and a smile.

"Me too. Thanks for your help. I need to get back to work."

"I should too, but I'd rather stay here and ogle the cutie behind the counter," Justus said.

Cael shook his head with a laugh as he left the shop. He knew he didn't have to check with Novi to see if she liked the idea of the steak house, because she'd told him she wanted to be surprised.

And he was definitely hoping to surprise her in more ways than one.

CHAPTER SEVEN

As Novi got ready for work on Tuesday, she mulled over what to say to her mom. Novi was working until four, and then Cael was picking her up for their date at six. She had no idea what he was planning because she'd asked him to surprise her. All she knew was that she should dress casually. On Monday, she'd found a cute denim mini skirt in the donation bin at the store, and matched it with a turquoise top with short, ruffled sleeves. The clothes hung in her closet, freshly washed and ironed.

Despite being ready to see Cael again—more than ready, actually—she hadn't told her mom anything yet. Not about the safari tour or meeting Cael or the hours they'd spent on the phone talking since meeting on Saturday. She was head over heels for him, and she'd only spent a couple hours in person with him. She couldn't shake the feeling that they were fated to meet, that he was her Mr. Right, and there was an answering echo of contentment within that part of her that felt feral.

And there was something Cael had said to her the day they met that she hadn't been able to shake.

He'd asked if she took after her father physically.

At the time, she'd thought he might mean the growling and other odd physical stuff, but she'd convinced herself that he must mean did she actually look like her father. But now, she was almost one hundred percent sure that Cael knew there was something different about her and it was related to her father. She just wished she could talk to her mom about that without her freaking out.

It begged the question—was there something different, really different, about her father that she'd inherited?

Was the part of her that felt like a feral barn cat when she got emotional more than just simple emotions?

She wanted to confide in Cael, but she was afraid he'd think she was nuts. And what would she say anyway? That she thought her dad was part animal and she'd inherited some of it too?

Shaking her head, she finished tying her tennis shoes and grabbed her phone from the dresser.

Taking in a deep breath, she opened her bedroom door and walked into the kitchen to find her mom stirring honey into a mug of steaming tea and looking at her phone.

"Morning," Novi said. She grabbed an apple from the bowl on the counter and sat, rubbing the shiny skin and thinking about what she would say.

"Hello, did you sleep well?"

"Not particularly."

"Oh?" Her mom looked up at her. "What kept you up?"

This was it. It was tell her now or keep hiding the truth.

"I met a guy."

"At work?"

"No...at the park."

Her mom's brows dropped down, a wrinkle forming between them. "What park?"

For a moment, Novi didn't say anything, but she decided

47

in that split second that she didn't want to hide anything from her mom about Cael because she liked him, and she thought there might be more there than just a guy she could date for a while and have fun with.

She thought Cael might be her future.

"I went to the safari park on Saturday afternoon, and after the tour, I met a guy named Cael there. He's the vet for the safari animals. We ate dinner together, and he took me into one of the paddocks to meet Tank, the park's mascot, and we've been talking on the phone ever since."

The words rushed out of her like a dam breaking, and she inhaled deeply to catch her breath when she was done.

Her mom said nothing, just stared at her with the same brown eyes Novi had herself.

"I told you it wasn't safe," her mom said finally. "Places like that use photos for publicity all the time. Your father could see your picture and know where we are."

"Mom, we haven't seen him in almost two years. We've moved three times since then, and there's no reason to think he's watching advertisements for a safari park on the East Coast." Novi rubbed her temple. "Aren't you tired of running? Because I am."

"For a guy." Her mom's brow arched, her gaze boring into Novi.

"Yes. No. Not just him. But I really like him."

"You don't know him."

"I know enough about him to know I want to see where it goes. I don't want to fall in love with him and then have to disappear because we may or may not still be on my father's radar."

Yes, she was very sure her father was dangerous. He'd made that abundantly clear. And there was also the pesky little fact that he didn't think Novi should even be alive.

"Do you think there's something different about him?" Novi blurted out.

"Who?"

"My father."

Her mom's brows furrowed. "What do you mean?"

"I mean *really* different. Like not..." She let the sentence die. Was she really going to say she wanted to know if her mom thought her dad wasn't fully human? It was too incredible to consider. But then she thought about how she felt when she was around Cael. That rumbly part of her liked him. A lot. Maybe even loved him a little already.

Novi pushed her hair back from her face and said, "I just want to stay, Mom. I don't want you to be afraid anymore. *I* don't want to be afraid. I feel safe with Cael, and I think you'll like him too. I know you will, because you love me, and you want me to be happy. Did you really think that we could live our entire lives without actually living? Aren't you ready for more, for better than just existing and always watching over our shoulders?"

Her mom went silent again, and Novi wanted to let out a growl in frustration.

"He...um..." Her mom cleared her throat. "He purred. Or growled, I guess. When we were...together." Her cheeks pinked and she averted her gaze. "I thought he was playing at being a tough guy, I even told him I thought he sounded like a cat. He got offended, but then he laughed and said he was just a growly guy by nature. When I told him I was pregnant, he was mad. He accused me of lying to try to trap him. His eyes changed color. They went from brown to pale blue—it was so startling that I never forgot it. When he tried to snatch you when you were two, his fingernails were black and sharp, and he had fangs in his mouth. I was terrified. I see that image in my dreams, of him trying to slash at you while my sister and I fought him back and kept you safe." She touched her arm and lifted her sleeve, showing Novi a set of scars on the underside of her arm. "He grabbed me. I wrenched my arm away and got these. I told you they were from a childhood pet, but they were from your father."

Novi stared mutely at her mom. She'd never told her so much about him.

Keir.

"But to answer your questions," her mom continued, "yes, I'm tired. Tired of running, tired of being scared. But I'll never stop wanting you to be safe. You think because we haven't seen him that we're safe, but I don't know if we are. I'm afraid to lose you. He wanted you dead, Novi. He's come after you more than once."

"Mom, I feel safe with Cael."

"Why? Because he's good-looking?"

"I never said he was."

Her mom rolled her eyes. "I'm sure he is."

"Well, yeah, he is, but that's not why. I feel connected to him in a way I can't really explain. I miss him terribly and I want to see him again." She rubbed the space over her heart. "Whatever my father is, whatever...other thing is within him, it's in me too. And I think it's why I want to be with Cael. He might be my forever guy."

"Might be?"

"I don't want to jinx it."

Her mom snorted and then closed her eyes with a groan. "I need to know that if I feel we're in danger, if I truly sense it, that you'll trust me."

"Of course I trust you."

Her mom opened her eyes, leveling a serious look at Novi. "Maybe this man of yours will keep you safe; that's what I've always wanted. I know you've been lonely all these years with just the two of us. You were bound to meet a man at some point, so I'm not surprised. I *am* surprised that you defied me, but I'm not mad. I'll want to meet him, of course. If you're going on a date, then you need to go about it the right way. I expect him to come to the door for you and to meet me." She narrowed her gaze. "Does he know?"

"Yes."

"Even your tendencies that are like your father's?"

"Yeah."

"I hope you've placed your trust in the right man, Novi, I truly do. I once trusted a man, and it put a target on my back. While I wouldn't trade you for anything in the world, I do wish that we hadn't been in danger all this time."

"Maybe my father's moved on," Novi said, sounding more hopeful than she actually felt.

"I guess we'll see."

Novi smiled and stood, then hugged her mom. "Thank you."

"You're welcome. Just be careful."

"I will, I promise."

Novi left for work, her steps feeling lighter than they had in years. She had a date and her mom's blessing, and she'd learned a lot more about her father. While things were still a mystery, she thought she could tell Cael and he'd understand. Maybe there was even something more to him than met the eye too. She certainly thought there might be, otherwise why would she feel so connected to him after such a short time?

Novi fiddled with her hair, growling in frustration as the braid she was attempting to use as a headband refused to cooperate. Finally, she twisted the offending locks away from her face and clipped them, fingering out the soft curls she'd placed at the bottom of her long hair.

She'd been on dates before, but she never dated a guy

more than a few times because of her mom's insistence that she not get too close to anyone when they might have to leave suddenly. This date with Cael felt so different, though.

Monumental.

She heard a car door shut outside, and her heart clenched. Cael!

Giving herself a once-over, she left the bathroom and quickly walked into the family room. Her mom looked up at her and said, "You look very lovely."

"Thanks." She smoothed her trembling fingers down the front of her short skirt and tugged on the hem. "I'm nervous."

"I'm sure he is too."

There was a knock at the door, and Novi smiled at her mom and then hurried to the door. After a quick peek through the peep hole to ensure it was him, she opened the door and her breath caught in her chest.

He was just so damn sexy.

Tall and broad, and stacked with muscles. And those eyes! Gray...no wait, they were brown. Like the elephant's eyes.

In that moment, she put two and two together and realized that he was like her and her father, not just a man but more.

Instead of being freaked out by that news, she was bolstered by it. It meant Cael would understand what she was feeling. And maybe he could even guess what her father was and help her understand what she was dealing with.

Cael held out a bouquet of colorful daisies and said, "You look amazing, Novi."

"Hi Cael," she said, thanking him for the flowers. He kissed her cheek, and she turned to the side and said, "Come in and meet my mom."

He stepped inside, and she shut the door. "Mom, this is Cael Donnelley. This is my mom, Lori Jones."

Her mom stood as Cael crossed the small family room to

greet her. After they shook hands, she said, "Have a seat, Cael. It's nice to meet you."

Cael sat on the couch opposite her mom, and Novi took the flowers and hurried into the kitchen to find a vase. She dusted one off from under the sink and filled it with water, listening as her mom and Cael exchanged pleasantries. She wondered if her mom would come right out and ask him, but she didn't let on that she and Novi's conversation that morning had been so serious.

"What made you want to be a vet?" her mom asked as Novi came back into the room with the flowers.

"I love animals. I always wanted to work with them. When I came to work at the safari park when I was eighteen, they put me to work in the paddocks cleaning and feeding the animals, and it just seemed natural to go to college to learn how to really take care of them."

"Sounds like you've got a nice setup there. Do you live near the park?"

"I do, actually. There's an apartment complex at the back of the park for staff."

Her mom nodded. "I should let you two get on your way. I've got plans to curl up with a good book."

"It was nice to meet you, Lori," Cael said as he stood and offered his hand to Novi. She took it and stood with him. "Night, Mom. I'll be quiet when I come in."

"Have fun," her mom said.

When Novi looked back at her mom as they headed to the door, she smiled and nodded her approval which made Novi grin.

When they were outside, Cael blew out a breath.

Novi chuckled. "That wasn't so bad, was it?"

"Just wait until you have to meet my parents. They're in Indiana, though, so you have a reprieve before that happens.

Maybe we can video chat soon though, I know they'd like to meet you."

"They would?"

Cael opened the passenger door of a large, white SUV, and she sat down. "Of course, sweetheart," he said, smiling down at her. "You're important to me. Why wouldn't they want to meet you?"

Novi smiled, feeling warm all the way through to the center of her being. He shut the door and came around to the other side, sliding behind the wheel. "You still want to be surprised, right?"

"Yep."

"Good. I won't make you close your eyes or anything, but I hope you like what I chose."

"I'm sure I will."

"I like your faith in me."

While he drove, she told him about the customer who'd come in and bought a dozen t-shirts to turn into yarn so she could make crafts, and the mother of three who was looking for shoes for her kids. He told her about tending to the giraffes and rhinos, and how Tank followed him around his paddock and made grumbly noises at him.

"What do you think he wanted?"

"I don't know, it's hard to say. Maybe more carrots."

"How did he come to the park?"

"Hunters came across his herd up north when he was young. He took a bullet to the leg and ran off. He was found by the side of the road by a man who had connections to an animal rescue in upstate New York. They didn't have room for him, but it's well known in the zoo community that we'll take certain animals in to care for them, so Alistair and I went to get him. He's been with us ever since."

"Aw, he lost his family though."

"He did, but I know he thinks of us as family, as well as

54

the animals in his paddock. He's really protective of Kelley's wife, Rhapsody. They just had a baby, and Tank recognized that she was pregnant and was really sweet with her."

"Kelley's one of your co-workers?"

"Yep."

He pulled to a stop in front of a Japanese steak house and turned off the engine. She let out a gasp. "I love these places. I haven't been to one since my mom's birthday last year. The guy tossed a shrimp at her and she freaked out and ducked, and it went flying onto another table."

He laughed. "I'm glad you're happy. I wanted something special for our first date."

He got out and came around to her side, opening her door and helping her out. He shut the door and looked down at her, curling his arm around her back and drawing her close.

"Novi."

"Yeah?"

"Did I tell you how beautiful you are?"

Her cheeks heated as she smiled up at him. "You're pretty sexy yourself."

"Then I'd say we're perfectly matched." He lowered his head, their lips nearly touching, and he whispered, "I fucking missed you, Novi."

And then he kissed her.

CHAPTER EIGHT

Since they were in a public restaurant and not alone at the table that surrounded their talented chef, Cael couldn't really talk to Novi about anything relating to what he was and what she might be, which made his elephant irritated. They'd already suffered without her for two nights, and the thought of a third night without her in their arms looming ahead was enough to make his beast want to riot.

But despite the fact that they kept their conversation light, talking about non-private subjects like work, hobbies, and favorite things, he felt like Novi's attitude had shifted since their first meeting. Something had changed her feelings toward him. It wasn't that he thought she didn't like him in the beginning, because he was sure she did, but she'd seemed hesitant and confused by her attraction to him.

Not anymore, it seemed.

She flirted and teased him, giggled and blushed, and every time her fingers grazed his skin his whole body jolted with awareness.

Her eyes, the beautiful dark brown that he'd memorized at their first meeting, slipped frequently to ice blue. The crinkles at the corners of her eyes when that happened told him that she wasn't fighting the change and was genuinely happy to be with him.

When they'd eaten their fill of steak and noodles, he paid the bill and took her hand.

"I notice we hold hands a lot," she said as they left the restaurant.

He chuckled. "I guess we do. Do you mind?"

"Not at all. I like it. It feels familiar and comfortable."

He unlocked the park's unmarked SUV and opened her door. "You haven't had that before."

She looked up at him, a flicker of sadness in her eyes. "No. It's just been me and Mom for so long."

"You don't have to be alone anymore, sweetheart. I'm here for you and I'm not going anywhere."

"Good."

She went onto her toes and kissed him. He wanted to chase her lips and devour her, but instead he smiled and shut her inside the SUV. "I've got another stop in mind," he said as he turned on the engine.

"Oh?"

"How about some ice cream?"

"I'd love that."

He texted Justus to let him know they were on the way to the ice cream shop. When they arrived, it was deserted save for the two workers behind the counter, and Cael was glad for that. He and Novi ordered sundaes—hers peanut butter and chocolate, and his caramel and pecans. They sat in a booth and were quiet for a few minutes as they dove into their desserts.

The door opened and Cael looked up, smiling as Justus and Trina walked in.

"Hey!" he said, lifting his hand and waving them over.

"What a nice surprise," Trina said, smiling.

"Novi, this is Justus and Trina, they work at the park. This is Novi."

"Nice to meet ya," Justus said, sticking out his hand.

Novi stared at him, her mouth open and her eyes wide.

Her blue eyes.

Her chest started to heave as she gasped for breath, panting as if she'd just run a marathon.

"Sweetheart?" Cael asked, his voice pinging with worry. He slipped from the booth and scooted in next to her, putting his arm around her. He tilted her chin up until she was looking at him. She looked panicked. "It's okay, they're my friends. He's my friend."

"I...I don't..." she gasped, her words coming out in harsh whispers.

"Don't be afraid," Cael said. "I told you I'm with you, I've got your back."

"Maybe we should go?" Trina asked, hooking her arm through Justus's and pulling him back a few steps.

"No, wait," Novi said. Her voice was a little deeper, her eyes a pale blue that was almost white. "I'm...I'm okay."

"If you're sure?" Cael asked.

She nodded, pursing her lips.

"We'll grab some ice cream and give you guys a chance to talk before we sit down," Justus said. "It's okay if you want us to leave, Novi, I promise."

She didn't take her eyes off Cael, her hands curling in his shirt.

When they were alone, Novi let out a breath and relaxed a fraction. She blinked rapidly, her eyes suddenly glittering with tears. "What's happening to me?"

"Tell me what it feels like."

"Like something's inside me and trying to come out," she whispered. Her voice was still low and deep, and he knew the humans behind the counter wouldn't be able to hear their conversation.

"Because of Justus?"

"Yeah. Do you know what's happening to me?"

"I believe so, but I don't think we should talk here."

She opened her mouth, closed it, and then her gaze darted from his toward the counter where Justus and Trina were paying for their ice cream.

She nodded in understanding.

Trina approached the table alone and Justus stayed back by the counter. "Would you like us to leave? Or we can sit at another table."

Novi dropped her head to Cael's chest and inhaled deeply. She relaxed another fraction and a soft growl reached his ears. "I don't know."

Cael chuckled and kissed the top of Novi's head. "It's okay, sweetheart, why don't we take off instead? We're done with our ice cream anyway."

"Okay. I'm sorry." She lifted her head and looked at Cael.

"Nothing to be sorry about."

"Maybe we can meet you guys later at the park?" Trina asked. "When we're not so exposed out in public."

"I'll text Justus and let you know," Cael said. He disposed of their trash and took Novi's hand, leading her out of the shop. When he shut her in the SUV, Justus met him on the sidewalk.

"Seems pretty obvious to me," Justus said, taking a bite of ice cream from a sugar cone. Trina was behind him, holding his hand and drinking a milkshake. "What do you want to do?"

"I'm taking her to the apartment complex. I'll see what she says and let you know if I need her to meet you again."

"We'll be available, whatever you need," Trina said.

"Thanks."

When Cael and Novi left the parking lot, he said, "I'd like to take you to my place."

"Okay. I heard you tell Mom you live at the park?"

"Yep." It was true and not true, but he couldn't tell her about the underground living space until he knew for sure wasn't going to run when she heard the truth. Their rule of thumb for revealing their shifter nature to humans was the human and shifter had to be in love and committed. Or, as was the case with Neo the gorilla and his human soulmate Dani, she guessed the truth.

Novi was quiet on the drive to the park, and he let her have the time with her thoughts. He'd grown up knowing about shifters of course, because he was one, but he couldn't imagine what was going through her head right then as she untangled years of wondering about her past and her father.

He used a code to unlock the security gate at the back of the park and took the road to the eight-unit apartment complex. He'd prepared earlier for the chance he might be able to bring her with him, so he'd gotten a key to unlock a unit, put some food in the fridge, clothes in the closet, and toiletries in the bathroom. She'd most likely guess that he didn't actually live there, but it was at least a place they could be together and that's what mattered.

He let her into the apartment on the second floor, flicking on the overhead light in the family room. Each two-bedroom apartment was furnished the same with a couch, coffee table, and TV in the family room, a table and chairs in the kitchen, and a king-sized bed in the master.

"This is nice," she said as she walked in and turned in a slow circle.

"I haven't been here long; they just finished the complex this winter. Would you like something to drink?"

"No." She faced him. "I just want you to tell me I'm not going crazy."

"You're not crazy, Novi, I promise. Tell me what you're thinking, no matter how off the wall you feel it is."

She put her hands on her hips and dropped her head to her chest. "I almost lost it in the ice cream shop. I mean, your friend smelled..." She lifted her head and looked at Cael, her eyes icy blue once more. "He smelled good. Not like you smell to me, like I want to roll around with you and get covered in your scent, but he smelled familiar. When I caught his cologne or whatever it was, it made everything in me react. It's how I felt when I met you, but not romantically. It was more like Justus felt like a part of my family. You just feel like everything to me."

Cael closed the distance to her and took her hands. Their fingers linked and he kissed her forehead. "You feel like everything to me too."

"My mom told me that my dad growled when they were together, and that she thought there was something different about him. Something... other. She never told me about that before, but because I told her today that I wanted to stay here and see where things go with you and not keep running, she told me more about him. I think that I'm more like my father physically than even she realized, but she doesn't know what it is."

"I thought you were acting different, like you'd had an epiphany."

"I did, I guess. And it had to do in part with the photo album."

"What about it?"

"The elephant that touched my hand? He was in the picture that Benjamin took. When I looked at the picture, I realized that the elephant's eyes were gray and not golden brown like they'd been in the beginning. Gray like yours."

Cael's eyes went wide. Holy shit. He wondered if that had ever been captured in a photo before and made a mental note to tell Alistair so that those in the office who handled the photos could be on the lookout for tell-tale signs of shifts.

"Your eyes change color when you get emotional. So do mine. Tell me what you think it means?"

The silence hung between them.

He wanted to urge her to speak her mind, but he didn't want to rush her. He couldn't make the jump for her, she had to do it herself. She had to admit that he was different and so was she.

She had to come to her own conclusions, and no matter how much he just wanted to come right out and say it, he couldn't.

"You're an elephant," she blurted.

Her cheeks went scarlet, and she sucked in a sharp breath.

He bit back a laugh. She looked adorably embarrassed.

Cupping her cheek he said, "Are you sure?"

She seemed to have been bracing for him to laugh in her face and tell her she was wrong, and when he didn't, her shoulders dropped and the tension she'd been holding eased. Straightening, she nodded vigorously. "You have the same color eyes. And when the elephant—you—touched me through the fence I felt a connection to him. When I met you in the office and you took my hand, that same connected feeling came over me. I didn't understand it, but I felt in my heart that we were meant to meet. And when you took me to the elephant paddock, there were only three of them in there and not four. Because you were with me and in your human body."

Relief swamped Cael. He was so happy that he wanted to whoop a cheer and dance.

Instead, he pulled her close and kissed her. She moaned softly and a growl rumbled in her chest.

She put her hands on his chest and leaned away from the

kiss. "So what is my father, then? Do you know? Oh!" Her eyes went wide. "Is Justus an animal too?"

"We're called shifters, sweetheart. And yes."

"What kind?"

"You said you felt a connection to him, not romantic but like family."

"Yeah.

"He's a bear. You smell like a bear to me, but it's subtle, like it's diluted. I think it's because you're only half-shifter, and not a full one as if you had two shifter parents. We have grizzly and black bears at the park, but you don't smell quite like them, so you may be a different species of bear."

"But I can't change into an animal. I just have these weird animal-type things like the growling and my fingers and teeth."

"Teeth?"

He led her to the couch, and they sat down.

"It all happens when I get emotional. My gums will ache, and my fingernails will turn black. Then there's my eyes of course, but not many people notice it."

"What about your mom?"

"When I was younger, I'd tell her when I felt strange and she'd freak out if I was around anyone. We'd end up moving since she was so worried that someone would come after me because I was different or that my father might hear about it. So I stopped telling her and tried to hide it. But I always felt so caged. Like I couldn't really be myself."

"That changed tonight, though. You weren't trying to hide it."

"It was a relief." She smiled at him and laid her head on the back of the couch. "My mom's still scared about my father. She's tired of being in hiding but she's willing to stay, so long as we're vigilant."

Cael had hoped to take Novi down to his home under the

park to live, but he doubted at this point she'd want to be away from her mom. It had been just the two of them her whole life, which must have felt so isolating. He glanced around the apartment and thought about the other empty ones. For tonight, he didn't need to worry about what the next steps in their relationship would be—although his elephant wanted to mate her immediately and start a family —he was just thankful that he didn't have to keep anything from her.

"I need to call Alistair," he said.

"Your boss? Why?"

"Because he's like me. So is Kelley, and there's one more you didn't meet—Indio."

"What about Kelley's wife?"

"Rhapsody's a black panther."

Novi's brows rose. "Panthers, bears, and elephants. Are there other types of shifters here?"

"Yep. We have five main groups—elephants, bears, lions, wolves, and gorillas. We also have a few individuals—a falcon, a red fox, and a horse. They're all mated except for the horse, he's the step-brother of a human who's mated to one of the gorillas."

"It's so incredible. I never would've guessed there are humans who can turn into animals. Even feeling the way I did all these years, I just thought something was wrong with me."

"You don't know about it because it's a closely guarded secret. You can't ever share this with anyone."

Understanding lit her features. "Not even my mom."

"I know it will be hard to keep it a secret from her, but it's imperative."

She put her hand up. "I get it. I totally understand. If humans knew there were people around who could turn into animals, they'd be scared and probably react violently. You need to keep the secret of the park safe." She got quiet, her brow furrowing.

Cael picked up her hand and kissed her knuckles. "What's wrong, sweetheart?"

"Is that why my dad tried to kill me? Why he's been hunting us?"

"I believe so. It's extreme, though. I've never known a shifter group to insist that a half-child born to one of their people needed to be killed. If one of our people had a child with a human unknowingly, they wouldn't try to take them out, they'd want them here where they could be safe and cared for."

"My life could've been so different if he'd just brought us into his group and taken care of us. What's a group of bears called?"

"It depends on the type. Black bears and grizzlies are sleuths, polar bears are a celebration. I wish you had been part of a bear group, hadn't been terrorized your whole life. I can't imagine how it felt to be on the run like that and never able to really settle in anywhere."

"I can settle in now, though."

"One hundred percent."

Her eyes flashed to blue and then back to brown, darkening slightly. "Cael?"

"Yes?"

She scooted a little closer, tilting her face up to kiss along his jaw. "Can I stay with you tonight?"

CHAPTER NINE

Novi had never been bold. In her head she always felt bold, but when it came to actually being bold, she always chickened out and got shy. But with Cael, she *was* bold. There was a relief that filled her because she could finally put the truth of her life together, could explain the strange things she felt and the way her body reacted.

And the mystery of why her father wanted her dead.

It angered her that she and her mom had been on the run for years to protect her simply because he hadn't used a condom. Or accepted responsibility for being a father and brought her and her mom into his life. She understood the need for secrecy, but there had to be a point where a life mattered more than the secret. She shouldn't have been on anyone's kill-list simply because of her paternity.

But here she was. Half human and half bear of some sort, if Cael's senses were reading her right.

She might never know the truth, but it suddenly didn't matter.

All that mattered was that Cael was with her and wanted to be with her... maybe? He still hadn't answered.

Cael cupped her face and brushed his lips over hers, sending a riot of sensations through her. "I want you to stay with me. I crave it. But we really shouldn't do more than just sleep if you're not ready to be with me."

"What do you mean?" She wrapped her hand around his wrist, anchoring herself to him.

"Shifters are prone to strong attachments when they find their mate. You're mine. Or, I want to ask you to be my mate officially. Once we have sex, my elephant is going to consider you our mate, our wife. We don't mark like some of the other shifter groups who will bite with their fangs to leave a permanent scar, but the intention is the same. Once I have you in my arms and in my bed, sweetheart, it's going to be impossible for me to let you go."

She let that roll around in her head. "You want me to move in with you, like tonight?"

"Maybe not tonight if we don't go any further than kissing and sleeping, but yes. Once we make love, my elephant won't be able to handle you sleeping anywhere else."

She was in a pickle. She really wanted to make love to Cael, and she even liked the idea of living with him. Hell, she was half in love with him already.

"When shifters meet their one right person—"

"Soulmate," he supplied.

"Right," she said and smiled. "When a shifter meets his or her soulmate, the instant connection that I felt with you is what you feel with me?"

"Absolutely. It's why I tried to keep you here at the park on Saturday for as long as possible. It made me feel down-right crazy to be away from you for two nights. But that being said, we don't have to do anything tonight. I'm content to have you here with me. We can move at whatever pace is right for us, the only expectation I have for tonight is that once I fall asleep, I'll get to wake up with you in my arms."

It was ridiculous how sweet he was. She was feeling supremely lucky.

"Do you still get married? If sleeping together makes a mating permanent, is marriage still done?"

"Yes. If the couple wants. Shifters choose mates in lots of different ways. A male might choose to have an arranged mating set up by his alpha or family, or a shifter couple might simply care for each other and want to get mated without being soulmates. But then there are shifters like me, who wanted to wait for our soulmate, the one person on the planet meant solely for us. I couldn't imagine going into an arranged mating. I waited...for you."

She felt like she was glowing from the inside out.

"I should text my mom and tell her I'm not going to be home."

He nodded and gave her a quick peck on the lips. "I'll speak to Alistair while you're doing that."

Novi sent a quick text to her mom. It was still early so her mom responded that she hoped she was being careful, and Novi promised she was and that she'd talk to her mom in the morning.

Cael was watching her when she put her phone on the coffee table and straightened.

"Alistair would like to meet us for breakfast in the employee cafeteria tomorrow," he said.

"Is everything okay?"

"Of course. He'd just like to hear you say in your own words what you know to be the truth, about yourself and me."

"Can I see you in your shift again? Not through a fence this time?"

He looked really pleased that she made the request. "I'd love that. Maybe after breakfast. We don't do VIP tours during the week, but there are tours in the afternoon, so we don't want to have you wandering around in the paddock without a uniform on."

"That would be strange for the tour guests for sure." She let out a breath and looked up at him.

Part of her wanted to move things forward physically and just move in with him, but the other part of her knew that it would be better to take things slow.

"I think I just want to sleep tonight," she said, toeing off her shoes. "I mean, I want you, no doubt about that, but I can't just move in with you without making sure my mom's okay with everything."

"And there are rules in the park for us, so I can't move into your place."

She chuckled. "That would've been handy. I'm worried Mom will be afraid to be alone. Or that she'll be worried about me."

"It'll work out, Novi, I promise. The good news is that we get to hold each other tonight, and I've been aching to do that since we met."

"Me too."

He took her hand and pulled her close, lowering his head slowly until their lips were almost touching.

He whispered her name.

"Yes?"

"Let's go to bed."

She grinned and threw her arms around his neck as he kissed her. Her toes curled as the kiss deepened and a happy rumble grew in her chest. He picked her up and carried her into the bedroom. He gave her a shirt of his to sleep in and went into the bathroom, coming out a few minutes later wearing track pants and nothing else, his sexy muscles on display.

She used the bathroom, brushing her teeth with a spare toothbrush. Tugging on the hem of the shirt which brushed the tops of her thighs, she smiled at her reflection. Her brown eyes flashed to blue, and she whispered to herself in the mirror, "I see you, she-bear, and I'm so happy you're part of me."

Her chest vibrated with a growl that sounded a bit like a purr.

She was the happiest she'd ever been, and she wasn't even planning to have sex with Cael tonight. She couldn't imagine how much happier she'd be once they were tangled together as lovers, and mated, and she was his and he was hers.

She opened the door to the bedroom and saw him sitting up against the pillows and leaning against the headboard.

"Come to bed, sweetheart," he said, patting the space next to him with a sweet smile. "Tomorrow's going to be a great day."

Keir Montague leaned back in the chair and looked at the report from his polar bear celebration's tracker. After nearly two years of chasing dead ends and rumors, Brandon finally found the bitch who'd consistently thwarted his attempts to right a wrong. His alpha had been pissed at Keir for two decades and refused to allow him to move up in the celebration and take his rightful place as second-in-command. And perhaps worse was that he wasn't allowed to take a mate until the mistake that had been born twenty-two years earlier was eradicated. No female would mate him while he was a marked male, and no alpha would support a mating between a female and a male like himself who'd made one grievous, drunken mistake.

He should've simply killed the human female when she'd sought him out with news of her pregnancy and been done with it. Then he wouldn't have suffered all these years, kept at a low-rank, refused even the basic right to take a mate and start a family. Keir had made a mistake, however. The protection he'd used had failed and the resulting child was part polar bear shifter and part human, and couldn't be allowed to live.

He had no parental bond with her, no familial attachment. He simply wanted the child and her mother dead so he could move the fuck on.

"You're certain it's them?" he asked, staring across the kitchen table at Brandon.

"One hundred percent."

The tablet showed a map with a star on the location of a house where the two were living. They were in New Jersey now. He'd lost track of them two years earlier. They were exceptionally good at staying off the radar. But now, fucking finally, he'd have the upper hand.

"Do you want me to put a crew together?" Brandon asked.

"I'll do it. You're dismissed."

Brandon nodded and left Keir's trailer, leaving him to his thoughts. He sent a text to his brothers—Donovan and Dorian. "It's finally time to set the past right. We leave in one hour."

His brothers replied they'd be ready.

Keir stood with a growl in his chest. He was so fucking ready to nail the coffin of his past shut so he could move the hell on to better things. Once the females were dead and his alpha had proof, Keir would finally take a mate and start a proper family. It was all he'd been wanting the past two decades, and it was all within reach.

He just needed to kill two people to make it happen.

Novi woke the next morning in Cael's arms, feeling more rested than she ever had in her life. While it had been tempting to take things all the way with him physically, they'd decided it was best to keep things as they were for now. They'd kissed and held each other several hours once they were in bed before drifting off to sleep with her tucked close against him.

She felt closer to Cael now that they'd shared so much. There was a freedom between them to talk about anything, because she knew his secret and he knew hers. She'd also learned that the park shifters lived in a huge underground compound with each group having their own private living quarters.

"Morning sweetheart," Cael said, kissing her shoulder.

She turned her head back to look at him with a smile and kissed him. "Morning."

"You look like you're thinking about something serious."

She turned to face him, resting her head on his biceps. "I was thinking about living arrangements."

"What about them?"

"Well, I guess more specifically I was thinking about living arrangements and my mom."

"I've had some thoughts about that as well."

"Oh?"

"I need to speak to Alistair, but I think that the alphas would be willing to let your mom move into one of these apartments. Since we can't tell her the truth of your father—or that shifters even exist at all—you and I could move in here. Then you'd still be close to your mom—we'd have our place and she'd have her own. That way we don't have to explain you live in the park but she can't come visit."

Novi let that roll around in her head. "Do you think she might someday figure out about shifters?"

"It's possible. She may already think it but feel it's too crazy to say out loud."

And Novi couldn't help her along with that knowledge. Cael had stressed to her how important the secret of shifters was. While she trusted her mom and knew her mom would never say anything to put anyone else in danger, Novi understood she was simply forbidden from telling her the truth in this matter.

"I like the idea of all of us living in the same complex. Can I see your real place, though?"

"Sure. Maybe after we meet Alistair I can show you around, and then you can help me with the norms if you want."

"Norms?"

"Normal, non-shifting animals."

"Is Tank really a shifter?"

"No, he's just a cranky, real moose."

"Are there moose shifters?" She sat up and stretched, her mind swirling with possibilities for different kinds of shifters.

"I've never met one, but who knows? Because we keep secret from humans, there are all sorts of shifters hiding in plain sight."

"So if you were out at a store or something and you smelled a shifter, you'd just ignore it?"

"It depends, I guess. It's honestly never happened, though. Well, aside from Dani's father and brother, who are horse shifters, but they smell human to us. If I was out in public and I scented another shifter, I'd be curious about them, but it wouldn't be like I'd out him or her to humans or something, that would be crazy. The shifters in our area all live in the park. Shifters by nature are territorial so they stick to their own areas."

"It's so strange to learn that there's this whole world I never even knew existed. It's too fantastical."

He chuckled and kissed her, then got out of bed. "We should get ready for breakfast."

His phone buzzed, and he picked it up from the side table and read the screen, then smiled as he typed. "There's a bag of clothes for you outside the door."

"There is? From who?"

"Trina."

"Aw, that's so sweet."

They checked outside the front door and found a paper sack which contained a pair of light gray leggings and a short-sleeved tunic in a buttery yellow. There were also a pair of flip flops and a bag of toiletries.

"Wow, this is so nice," Novi said as she looked over the items. "How did she know?"

"What, that you were staying here or that you'd appreciate clothes?"

"Both, I guess."

"I told Justus last night that you'd be staying with me in the apartment, and I'm sure she just assumed you didn't have any clothes with you."

"He's not an elephant but he cared about me because I'm your mate?"

"Yep. We all look out for each other."

Her heart clenched a little at the idea of having a big group of people from all different walks of life looking out for her because Cael was her guy. She loved that idea hard. And she thought her mom would love it too, once she got used to the idea of being around people and not staying in hiding. How long had it been since her mom had had a real friend besides her? They both deserved this.

"Thank you," Novi said, her eyes stinging with sudden tears.

"For what?"

"Just...thank you for everything."

Cael moved to her and gave her a tight hug. "Sweetheart, I'd do anything for you, up to and including giving you and your mom a safe place to live. You're everything to me, and I want us to have a long and happy life together."

"I want that too."

He tilted her face up to his and smiled at her. "Let's get to breakfast. The sooner we meet with my alpha, the sooner we can get on with the rest of our plans."

Suddenly she couldn't wait for that. Because she'd get to see him in his shift again. And then they'd....maybe come back here and see where the day took them.

Her gaze slipped to the unmade bed and her stomach flipped.

She couldn't wait.

CHAPTER TEN

Cael punched in the code to unlock the employee cafeteria and held the door open for Novi. Inside, a long table was set with breakfast items. Alistair was seated at the table, as was Joss and his soulmate, Jeanie, and the bear alpha, Marcus. Cael introduced Novi, who shook hands with everyone and got a hug from Jeanie.

"Have a seat," Alistair said, gesturing to the empty chairs across the table from him.

"Thanks," Cael said as he pulled Novi's chair out for her.

"Before we get to the meal," Joss said, clearing his throat, "we wanted you to tell us, in your own words, Novi, what you know about Cael and the park."

Novi nodded. She spoke softly at first, her voice touched with nerves, but the longer she spoke, the more confident and animated she grew. She told her whole story, ending with the connection she felt to Cael and the truth she now knew about her father and herself, as well as shifters in general.

The room fell into silence when she finished, and she looked to Cael with raised brows.

"You did great," he whispered, and kissed her cheek.

"You did," Alistair said. "Your story is...well, it's frankly a miracle that your mother was able to keep the two of you hidden for so long, particularly from a predator like a bear shifter."

"I'm thankful every day for all the sacrifices she did to keep us both safe."

"You've no idea why he's after you, though?" Joss asked.

"No," Novi said, shaking her head. "From what I've learned from Cael about soulmates, I don't think that's what he's feeling toward my mom. I mean, I don't think he's chased us for twenty years because he's in love with her. I think it's because I'm part whatever sort of bear he is. He has no evidence that either of us even know about shifters, and he'd know by now that we haven't told anyone the secret about shifters. If it was because he was afraid we'd tell, I think we've proved all this time that we're really good at keeping secrets."

"Indeed," Alistair said. "And you're certain your mom doesn't know?"

"I think she knows there's something different about him, and about me, but if she believes people can turn into animals she's never shared it with me."

"You and your mom must be so scared," Jeanie said.

"It's been a tough life," Novi admitted. "But I wouldn't change the journey that brought me and Cael together. I hate everything about the way my father has treated us, but without the constant moving from area to area, we wouldn't have come to New Jersey and I wouldn't have met Cael."

Cael grinned.

"How long has it been since you've seen your father or any evidence that he's still after you?" Joss asked.

"Almost two years. I told Mom that I thought it was time for us to settle down, but she's always got one hand on the go-bag, watching and worried that he'll show up and she won't be ready to get away."

The alphas went quiet again, and Jeanie said, "Let's eat before everything gets cold. I think our alphas have a lot to talk about."

The bears handled the food, from the stands in the park to the cafeteria to the market in the center of the underground living space. Cael wasn't one to do much cooking, so he normally took his meals in the cafeteria and market, but now that he and Novi were going to be living in the apartment, he'd have to change that. The bears had set the table with trays of food—breakfast sandwiches and wraps, hashbrown patties, and individual bowls of fruit. The males all waited for Novi and Jeanie to fill their plates, and then they set into the food. Male shifters ate a lot, their beasts burned off calories at a high rate. Cael didn't think there would be much in the way of leftovers once they were finished.

While they ate, the alphas explained the park operations to Novi and how it had become a haven to them, enabling them to keep the secret of their shifts.

Novi settled back in her chair and picked up her second cup of coffee. "It's amazing. I don't know how the secret's been kept all these years, I mean you're not the only shifters in the world, but humans don't have a clue. Not really, anyway. There are always myths and legends, but most people don't put stock in them."

"We're careful," Alistair said. "All our people are. We've had some slipups here and there, but fortunately nothing major has gotten out to the public."

Cael thought back to the "slipups," which included Win the gorilla falling asleep at his soulmate Lexy's place and shifting while they slept. It could easily have made their secret public if he hadn't been able to convince her to keep things between them.

"I promise I understand why you need to live in secrecy, and I wouldn't do anything to endanger Cael or any of you."

"Good," Alistair said. "Until you're officially mated, however, you won't be allowed to live underground with our people. Cael mentioned that the two of you could stay in the apartment complex and had asked if your mother could also have an apartment. The alphas have discussed it, and we'd like to offer an apartment to her."

"That's so nice, thank you," Novi said. "I'm just not sure how to broach the subject with her."

"What do you mean?" Cael asked.

"Well, honestly, how often does a guy meet a girl and a few days later asks her to move into his apartment, and also makes arrangements for her mom to have a place to stay in the same complex? It's...I don't know, it's unbelievable."

"Good point," Cael said. "Since we can't tell her about our people, we can't say that taking care of her is part of my nature—you're my soulmate and that makes her family to me, to the memory."

"What do you do for work?" Joss asked Novi.

"I work at a thrift store. It's mostly logging and sorting donations and dealing with customers. Why?"

"We heard about the photo album mishap," Joss said. "I was just thinking that we could use a dedicated person to print out the albums and look for that kind of thing, as opposed to having whoever is in the security office put them together."

"What mishap?" Novi asked.

"My eye color change in the picture of you and me when I was an elephant. We're not sure it's happened before, but it's something to watch out for in the future."

"You want me to work at the park?" she asked, looking at Cael first and then the alphas.

"A lot of the soulmates work here," Jeanie said. "I joined

the bears on the cooking team, Trina and Lexy work in the candy shop, Adriana and Celeste work in the market at a nail salon, and Dani has a makeup studio, Devlin works in finance, and Rhapsody helps out with the norms."

"You forgot about the bird sanctuary," Marcus said. "Auden and his soulmate Jess oversee it. And Tayme and Rory handle the ice cream stall in the park."

"Wow," Novi said. "That's pretty neat. I've only been working at the thrift store for a few weeks, so I'd be willing to work at the park and do the albums or whatever else needs to be done."

Cael was thrilled that his sweetheart was going to be able to work in the park. He'd get to see her whenever they were free, and he'd know that she was in the security office which was one of the safest places to be.

"Then it's settled," Joss said. "We'll need you to fill out an employment application for the files, it's just a formality."

"We'll figure out something for you to tell your mom," Alistair said. "That way you'll know she's safe."

"Thank you. Thanks for everything," Novi said.

"I'd like to show her my place underground and grab a bag of clothes to take to the apartment, and then I was hoping to let her see me shift," Cael said.

"Sounds good," Joss said. "Just be sure she's wearing a uniform out in the paddock."

"Of course."

Marcus said, "I think your father is probably a polar bear."

Everyone looked at him, and he shrugged with a smile. "Justus said he didn't know what kind of bear you were, and Alistair asked me to join you for breakfast this morning, not only to meet you but hopefully to figure out what you are exactly. All bears smell similar, but each species has a different scent so to speak. So grizzlies smell the same and black bears do, but they don't smell quite like each other. I met a polar bear through a mutual friend when I was in high school, and while your scent is light since you're only half shifter, it reminds me of how he smelled."

Novi hummed. "Are there are a lot of polar bears around?"

"None that we know of in New Jersey," Marcus said. "Shifter groups keep to themselves mostly. Our situation in the park is pretty unusual with so many different groups living and working together."

"My father's home is in Iowa, but he's been trying to find us for so many years, I've often wondered if his home base is still there or if it's moved."

"Bears like to hunker down in one area and claim it for a territory, particularly if it's away from humans. I doubt he's moved. He's probably using his own people to hunt for you."

"Hopefully once you get out of your place," Cael said, "you and your mom won't have to worry about him anymore."

"I hope so too."

"We'll continue to be vigilant, though," Joss said. "We take the safety of everyone in the park very seriously. You'll want to meet with Jupiter, since he's head of park security. She'll need an ID badge."

"We'll take care of that today, after the other stuff on our list."

Joss nodded. Jeanie came around the table and gave Novi another hug and handed her a scrap of paper with her number on it. "Send me a text and let me know your number. You can call me anytime for anything you need."

"Thank you."

Novi tucked the number into her phone case and looked at Cael. "I'm ready when you are."

"Excited to see a certain elephant?"

"You know it."

After they said their goodbyes, he took her down to the

private living quarters and to his home. She sat on the bed and watched as he packed a duffel. "It's really nice down here," she said. "I'm sorry you have to give it up because of me."

"Even if we were mated, since you want your mom to live in the apartments, it would be hard to explain why she can live there but you and I don't without her wondering where you were anyway. Besides," he said, cupping her face and giving her a kiss, "I get you. I could care less where we're living so long as we can be with each other."

She reached for him, but he took a step back with a laugh. "Sorry sweetheart, you're addictive and you want to see me shift. If we get distracted, we'll never leave."

"Good point. I can't help it that you're addictive too."

They hit up the norm paddocks first, both donning uniforms. It took a few hours to feed and check on the animals, but he loved having her by his side while he worked. She was a hard worker and curious about everything he did, and he was happy to share his knowledge with her.

They finally reached the elephant paddock. He set his duffel on the worktable in the shed and turned to face her.

"I can't wait to see you," she said. Her tone hinted at sex, curiosity, and lust mixed up together.

He undid the top of the uniform as he toed off his boots. He put his thumbs inside the lower part of the uniform and grinned as her gaze dropped to follow his hands.

"Hey, my eyes are up here," he said, pointing to his face.

She jerked her head up, her cheeks pinking. "You're too sexy."

"You are too. But if you keep looking at me like you want to lick me from head to toe, I'm not going to be able to shift because my human body is going to be fighting the change."

She took a step to him, her body brushing against his. "I

feel like things have changed between us because I know the truth now. Do you?"

"One hundred percent. I think you felt like I was holding something back from you, even though I really didn't have a choice."

"I did. And I couldn't really explain why I felt so close to you so fast. Now I know that it's in part because the bear side of me is crazy about you."

"I like that you're calling her your bear side."

"I used to just think of myself as having a feral side, some weird animal traits that I couldn't explain. I guess the human mind is good at making up excuses for that kind of thing and glossing over stuff that doesn't make sense."

He cupped her face and let out his elephant's version of a growl, a low, grumbling sound. "I'm crazy about you too, Novi. I'm so glad you're here."

She wiggled her fingers between his uniform and skin, and twisted, undoing a button. Her breath fanned his face as she smiled. "Get naked, sexy man. I want to see your elephant, and then I want to go to our new home and lock the door for a couple of days."

His elephant couldn't decide what was better—showing her their shift or staying human so they could take her to bed. But he won that argument, because she wanted to see him in his shift and it was important to him that she know what it really was like to change. Because she was only half shifter, she'd never have the ability to change forms. But she could commune with him and that's what counted.

She undid another button, her smile slipping from sweet to sultry. He let out a laugh which came out sounding a lot more choked than he'd planned, and extracted her nimble fingers as they attempted to slide farther inside.

"You're dangerous, sweetheart," he said.

"Only in the sexiest way." She winked, and he shook his head as he finished stripping.

"I'll remember this teasing later."

"Uh oh."

"Ready?"

She nodded, her eyes alight with curiosity. It took a moment for his human side to settle from the illicit thoughts traipsing through his brain, but his elephant took over and his shift came over him. He didn't take his eyes off her as he changed forms, from two legs to four with a huge trunk and white tusks. He shook out his ears and bumped into the table behind him, rattling the items on it.

"Holy shit."

He let out a chuckle, a blast of air from his trunk.

"You're...oh my gosh. You're an elephant." She reached out a trembling hand and he didn't move, letting her come to him and lay her warm hand on his trunk. She grew bold quickly, stroking his trunk and moving to his side where she touched his front leg. He lowered his head and hooked his trunk around her waist lightly, and she laughed.

"I mean, in my head I knew you were an elephant, but seeing this in person is...holy shit. I think I said that already, but it's really the most apt phrase I can think of. Incredible. You're just so amazing." She came around to the front of him, and he could see tears glistening in her eyes.

He made a curious sound, and she sniffled. "I'm okay, I promise. I'm just so amazed. And honestly, I feel so connected to you right now. It's like seeing you change forms has opened up something inside me. I feel at peace and happy. My bear does too." She pressed her forehead to his trunk and let out a trembling breath. He was fully humbled by her words and wished he could tell her he felt the same way.

And he would, when he was back to human.

She moved to the big doors and pushed them open. They were heavy, so he helped, swinging them wide so he could lumber out with her. He looked down at her, and she lifted her face to his.

"I guess we can walk around?"

He nodded.

She lifted her hand and he hooked his trunk around it, smiling inwardly as they slowly walked the perimeter of the paddock, finding shade under a tree. He settled down on the ground, and she curled up against him.

"In my wildest dreams I don't think I could've imagined being in this place, but it feels so right. I feel at home with you. I feel like I'm finally where I'm supposed to be."

He murmured in agreement.

"Well, I'm not going to say any more serious things until you can speak again." She snuggled down a little deeper and yawned. "This is so kick ass."

It totally was.

CHAPTER ELEVEN

By the time they were walking back to the maintenance shed where Cael could change back into human, Novi was fully head over heels for him, and also crazy turned on. She couldn't wait to see him back in his human form again.

Pulling the doors shut once he was inside, she flipped on the overhead light and watched as he quickly transformed from huge elephant to sexy human.

He rolled his neck with a sigh and then turned to face her. She'd had a good time ogling his butt, but she liked the front of him a whole heck of a lot too.

He gave her a curious smile.

She had a hundred things she wanted to say to him, but she couldn't decide what to start with, so she simply closed the distance between them, wrapped her arms around his neck, and kissed him. He let out a happy hum and she grinned, kissing her way from his lips across his jaw.

He lifted her up and set her on the counter, their lips meeting again. He pulled her flush against him, his fingers flexing on her knees. She could feel the hard, hot length of him between her legs, and she ached all the way to the center of her being.

Their lips parted and their tongues slid together, her stomach twisting pleasantly.

Her breath heaved in her chest as he eased back and smiled, his eyes flashing from gray to brown. "The others will be up here soon to shift and be out in the paddock for the group tours, so we can't do anything here."

"I don't want to wait anymore," she said, wrapping her hands around his wrists. "I want to be yours."

"You are."

"I mean, I want to be your mate. Officially."

He gave her a long, quiet look. "Are you sure? Once we go forward physically, once we make love, I won't be able to be apart from you at night. You'll need to move in with me."

"I know. I'm ready for that. I don't want to be away from you. Once we figure out what to do about my mom, I know she'll move in here. But even if she doesn't, I still want you. I want to build a life with you, here, and stay."

"Then let's go down to my house. It's closer."

She grinned at his eagerness. He hurriedly tugged his uniform on and grabbed his duffel from the table. She hopped to the floor and followed him down the stairs to the elephants' private living quarters.

He opened the door to his house and let her in. He locked the door behind them and set his duffel on the floor.

"I have a question for you," he said as he took her hands and gazed at her with adoration in the gray depths. "Would you be my mate, Novi? Would you move in with me here in the park?"

She grinned. "Yes."

He hooked an arm around her and drew her against him. "I'll ask you to marry me too, but for now you're mine and

I'm yours, and that's what matters. After this, there's no going back."

She nodded. "For both of us."

He lifted her into his arms and carried her to the bedroom.

As he set her on the bed, she pulled him with her, twisting until he was underneath her. She straddled his waist with a mischievous smile and leaned forward to kiss him.

He slid his hands up her sides slowly, curving them around to the front of the uniform. The kiss deepened and she let out a soft moan as he undid the buttons and pushed the garment from her shoulders. She eased from his lips reluctantly and wiggled out of the top of the uniform. Letting her fingers glide down the front of his uniform, she undid his buttons and spread the material apart, smiling at the taut muscles that were revealed. He was so sexy, even in a drab uniform.

She slid from the bed and took off the rest, her gaze hungrily taking in Cael's motions as he maneuvered the material off his own body. A moment later, they were back in each other's arms, clad only in their undergarments, and she sighed happily at the contact. She straddled his lap, letting her fingers roam over his shoulders and down his arms as they kissed again. She kissed her way down his throat, nipping at the pulse that thundered under her tongue. She had the sudden desire to bite him there, and she paused, thinking about the strange urge. Fairly certain it was her bear telling her to bite him, she pushed the thought from her mind.

He settled on his back at her urging, and she made her way down his chest, kissing and licking and tasting every inch of him. His cock peeked from the waistband of his boxer briefs, and she scooted down and tugged the thick length free from the soft material.

He sucked in a hard breath as she slowly licked around the head. She slowly took him into her mouth as far as she could, and his back bowed as he let out a grunt and tangled his fingers in her hair. She eased him from her mouth with the same deliberate slowness, keeping her gaze locked on his as she dove down once more.

He clenched his teeth together, his eyes flashing to the brown of his elephant. His whole body shuddered as she let him slide from her mouth.

He stopped her, letting out a harsh breath. "I don't want to come without you. It's too good, too much. Come up here, let me take care of you."

His finger crooked and she grinned, kissing the tip of his cock and wiggling from her panties. She climbed up his body, and he grabbed her hips and lifted her over his mouth. She settled her knees on either side of his head and grabbed the headboard for balance.

Looking down at him, she wanted to tell him how much she cared for him, how right this all felt.

Then he swiped his tongue up her folds and every single thought in her mind fled.

He parted her with his fingers, finding her clit and flicking his tongue over it a few times, just enough to ratchet up her desire. He tongued her core, sliding his tongue in and out. She groaned as heat flooded through her. Her body tingled, her breath coming out sharp and loud. She buried her fingers in his hair and clenched them, pleasure seeping through her as he closed his lips around her clit and sucked. His tongue moved over her, finding all the spots that made her feel like she was going to melt from the inside out.

Heat swelled within her, her body locking up as her climax struck. She threw back her head and shouted his name, the bear part of her wanting to growl in happiness. That sound spilled from her lips as he pushed her to another climax, his fingers slipping into her wet heat and driving her wild. Her body clenched hard around his fingers, and she couldn't do anything but hold onto the headboard for dear life.

He moved so fast that he was underneath her one moment and behind her the next, his hands curling around her hips as he placed his cock at her entrance and drove home.

Her teeth clicked together as her head kicked back. He filled her so completely, so perfectly.

Cael kissed her neck, his warm breath skirting over her skin.

"Fucking perfect," he said hoarsely, his fingers digging into her skin.

She would've agreed, but her tongue was glued to the roof of her mouth and her body was still spiraling with pleasure.

Pulling from her slowly, he plunged back in, setting up a fast rhythm. The headboard banged against the wall as she gripped it tightly.

He slid his hand up the front of her body, tugging her bra down to release her breasts. He played with her nipples, tugging and pinching them gently as he drove her to another great height of pleasure.

She chanted his name, her gums tingling and her fingertips aching as her bear grew loud and demanding.

She didn't know what the beast wanted.

No...wait...she did.

She gripped his head and pulled him forward, turning to place her lips on his neck.

"Yes, Novi, yes," he said, groaning.

She bit his neck. Hard. Her gums tingling even more, her head filled with the desire to mark him so everyone would know that he was hers.

He let out a shout as she released his neck, thrusting into her a few more times before he stilled, buried deep inside her.

She felt his cock spasming, felt the heat of his come.

Her whole body felt electrified, her heart pounding and her bear content.

Cael kissed her neck and groaned as he pulled from her depths. He dropped to the bed, taking her with him. She curled up in his arms, her skin tingling and her heart soaring.

"I love you," he said, at the same time she said it to him.

They both laughed, their gazes locked together, and their hearts aligned.

"I do, sweetheart," he said.

She lifted her head to brush her lips against his. "I do too. Mate."

"Mate."

They made love a second time, and then decided that it was too late to go to the apartment. She was happy to be in the house underground. It felt so safe and so much like home. Her whole life, home had been a relative term. She thought of her mom as home, that wherever her mom was...that was home. But now that she was with Cael, she knew home wasn't just a person, because for sure Cael had her heart and was home for her, but it was a place too. A place of warmth and love and security.

They fell asleep tangled together, her last thought was how crazy in love with her soulmate she was, even though it had only been a few days. She didn't understand it, but she knew it was real and true. She couldn't wait to see what the future would bring.

CHAPTER TWELVE

Cael woke slowly, aware that his sweetheart was sprawled across him like a warm blanket, her breath fanning across his chest. He'd honestly never been happier. Not only had she said yes to being his mate, but while they'd made love, she bit him, the part of her that was a bear wanting to mark her mate. His neck had throbbed under her blunt teeth, but she hadn't been able to break the skin. It didn't matter, though, he'd wear the bruise with pride for as long as it lasted with his fast healing.

And, even more amazing, was they'd declared their love for each other.

He'd never been in love before. He was glad that Novi, his soulmate, was the first female to ever have his heart.

Novi stirred and rubbed her cheek on his chest as she yawned.

He kissed the top of her head, and she tilted her face to his, giving him a sleepy smile. "Morning," she said.

"Good morning. It's still early, you don't have to leave for work for about an hour."

She made a face. "I'm not looking forward to giving my two weeks' notice."

"You've moved a lot, though. Haven't you given your notice frequently in the past?"

"Yeah." She sat up and stretched. "But it's always hard when I like a place, and I do like the manager at the thrift store and looking through all the stuff people donate."

She told him that she loved old books. But because they moved so much, she'd never been able to keep a lot of them. He decided he wanted to build her as many bookshelves as she needed to keep every book she wanted. Of course, they would be living in the apartment now, and probably for the conceivable future. He thought it was possible that her mother would never come to know the truth about shifters, and if that were the case, they wouldn't be able to live under the park.

Which would be a bummer. He couldn't see raising a family in the apartment. It was nice, but it was only two bedrooms.

She touched the corner of his mouth. "Are you okay?"

"Yeah." He scrubbed a hand over his face and sat up. "I was just thinking about having a family."

Her eyes crinkled as she smiled. "How many kids would you like?"

"I'm an only child, so I always wanted to have a couple of siblings."

"Me too. I was always jealous of kids that had brothers and sisters. So maybe three kids?"

"That sounds perfect. And we can get started right away," he said, wiggling his brows suggestively.

"We already did, remember?"

He did, of course. She wasn't on birth control, but they'd decided to make love anyway despite that fact. They were soulmates, and although she was half human, the part of her that was a shifter was ready to move forward, and that meant babies. They'd talked about the fact she could be pregnant already after the second time they made love, and they'd decided that whenever she did get pregnant would be the right time for them.

She bent and kissed him. "Dibs on the shower."

He laughed. "I could join you."

"Nuh uh. I'll be late to work if I see you all soapy and wet."

"I'm that irresistible, huh?"

"One hundred percent." She climbed from the bed and said, "I won't be long."

When the bathroom door was shut, Cael swung his legs around and grabbed his phone. He was going to drive Novi to work and then come back to the park and get to his duties. Then he'd pick her up when her day was finished and take her to her place so she could pack. He had no idea when she'd talk to her mom about moving in with him, but she promised she wasn't worried about her mom's approval.

He needed to tell his parents about his good news, and sent a text asking if they had time to video chat later that morning. He'd want to have them meet Novi via video chat later too.

They had just enough time to get to her work by the time they were both ready and walked to the employee lot where the park's SUVs were.

"You sure you don't mind driving me back and forth?" she asked as he opened the door to one of the unmarked SUVs for her.

"I don't mind, I promise." He shut her door and hurried around to his side, sliding behind the wheel. "And if you needed to, you could also just use one of the park vehicles."

"Why are some of the SUVs marked and some aren't?"

Half of the park's SUVs had large logos on the sides and back, and the others were plain.

"When Rhapsody and Kelley went to her place to pack after they mated, we only had marked vehicles, and they used one. It turned out that a male was stalking her in order to take her as his mate, and he was watching her house. He saw the park's information on the SUV and came for her."

"Scary. She's okay though, right?"

"Yep. It all worked out, but the alphas declared that if someone wasn't doing official park work, they needed to use an unmarked vehicle."

She hummed. "That's pretty smart."

"That's why they're the alphas."

"So who will be alpha when Alistair is finished?"

"I don't know, actually. I expect he'll be alpha until he dies or decides to retire. Elephants aren't like wolves that need ranks, so we don't have an official second-in-command. We'd probably vote on who took over, or Alistair might name his successor."

"Do you want to be alpha?"

"Nah, I've got my hands full being the only vet. Being alpha means meetings with the other alphas and being responsible for the safety of every shifter in the park, not just our people. I only want to be responsible for you and our children, and the animals."

He pulled into a spot near the front door of the thrift shop.

"I really don't want to go to work today," she said, brushing a lock of hair away from her face.

"I don't either, but we do what we must."

"Thank goodness in two weeks I'll be able to be in the park and we won't have to say goodbye like this and be apart."

"It'll be nice to see you whenever I want."

"I agree, I'm pretty fabulous." She shot him a big grin, and he chuckled.

"You are," he said.

Her eyes grew serious, and she said, "I'm going to miss you. But I'm excited for the day to be over so we can see my mom and pack up."

"That goes double for me." They kissed, and though he'd meant it to be quick so he didn't get too caught up in her, she was addictive in every form of the word, and the kiss grew deep really fast.

She pulled back with a little sigh. "So easy to get carried away."

"It really is. Have a good day, sweetheart. Love you."

"Love you too. See you at five."

She grabbed her pack and shouldered it as she climbed from the SUV. He waited until she was inside the building and had turned to wave at him. Giving her a wave in return, he turned from the parking lot and headed back to the park.

Once he'd arrived, he got a text from his parents that they were available for a video chat, so he called them from the maintenance shed while he prepped the food for the antelope, deer, and Tank.

"How are you, son?" his dad, Braden, asked.

"Great, Dad, you?"

"Could complain, but I won't. I'm breathing, the sun is shining, and I'm getting a new chair for my office on Friday."

"Sounds good. How are you, Mom?"

"Good, honey."

His parents weren't mated. They were part of the same memory that he'd grown up in, but aside from getting together to have him, they hadn't wanted anything more permanent. They were both hoping to someday find their soulmate.

"So the reason I wanted to talk to you guys is that I found my soulmate. Her name is Novi and she's human. Well, part human and part polar bear."

There was stunned silence for a long moment and then both his parents talked over each other as they congratulated him.

"Wait, did you say she was part polar bear?" his mom, Abigail, asked.

"Yeah. It's a crazy situation," he said, explaining how her life had been as she and her mom had stayed hidden from her father who was clearly off his rocker.

"That's terrible," his father said. "The male should've taken them both in instead of trying to kill her. I've never heard of that happening, but then again polar bears notoriously keep to themselves and tend to be old fashioned with lots of rules and traditions."

Cael nodded. "I think that's the case. He's following his group's rules and that's why he won't just leave them alone."

"She'll be safe with you in the park, though," his mom said. "That's the benefit of where you guys live. I'm not sure I could stand to live underground, but it does have its benefits."

"You get used to it," Cael said. "We're hoping to get Novi's mom to take one of the apartments here, so she'll be safer. Until she does, Novi and I will stay underground, and then we'll move up into the complex when she does."

"How are you going to get her into an apartment?" his dad asked.

"We're not sure yet. The alphas are trying to come up with a plausible explanation for why she can take one of them, but so far no one has any good ideas."

"I'm sure you'll come up with something," his mom said. "So when can we meet Novi?"

"I'd like to bring her to the memory in a few weeks maybe? But I was hoping we could all video chat tonight."

"That would be fine," his dad said. "Just send us a note to let us know when."

"You got it," Cael said.

"Can't wait to meet her," his mom said. "And we're so happy for you, honey."

"Thanks, Mom. Love you both."

His parents returned the sentiment and said goodbye. Cael smiled, thankful that his parents were happy for him. He'd known they would be. They wanted him to be happy, and they didn't care that Novi was human. Cael didn't care, either. He was glad she was in his life. Making love to her, waking up with her, had been heaven, and he had a lifetime of that to look forward to.

When he finished his work with the norms, he grabbed lunch in the employee cafeteria and met with Alistair to see if the alphas had any ideas.

"It would be handy if she would accept a job in the park and we could make the apartment part of her salary," Alistair said. "But we don't really have any openings that a human could fill without knowing the truth of what we are. So much about the park, and us, is secret and needs to stay that way."

"What would really be good is if Novi's biological father gave up and left them alone, so her mom could keep her place and be safe. But Novi's not happy with her being alone because she doesn't trust that her father won't show up at some point."

Alistair nodded, rubbing his chin. "It's unfortunate there isn't some kind of shifter location system, where we could find her father and preemptively state Novi and her mother are under our protection and he needs to forget about them."

Unfortunately, that wasn't going to happen. Shifters valued their privacy and keeping the secret from humans too much to do something so bold as to tell others where they were. Even if it was a private system for shifters, there were dangerous groups out there who would look at any kind of information like that as a way to take over territory or pull a coup and lead a group. Most shifter groups were on their own. The park was a unique place because the different groups all had each other's backs. Any group that came against one of the groups at the park would be taking on every single shifter inside.

"Well, no such luck with that," Cael said. "I'll come up with something to get her to the complex one way or another. She's my mother-in-law and I won't be able to rest easy until I know she's safe all the time."

"I understand. If I, or any of the alphas, think of anything that would be helpful, we'll let you know. In the meantime, what are your plans?"

"I'm picking up Novi and taking her to her place so she can pack, and then we'll come back here."

"You're going to stay underground until her mom moves in, assuming she ever does?"

"Yes."

"All right, keep me posted. We'd like to have dinner with you two, the whole memory. Rhapsody would like to get to know her better; she's excited to have another non-elephant person to hang out with."

Cael was glad that there was another female for Novi to get to know in the memory as well.

He said goodbye to his alpha and went to his house to get ready to pick up Novi. The closer it got to the time to see her, the more excited his beast became. She'd been on his mind all day, but now that it was near the time to see her again, he was thrilled with the prospect.

He parked in front of the thrift store and walked inside, curious about her work. She waved and smiled at him from behind the counter where she was checking out an older woman with a stack of clothes.

"Are you Cael?" an older woman asked.

"Yes. Are you Novi's boss, Katya?"

"I am," she said with a grin. "It's really nice to meet you, even though I'm disappointed that she's quitting to work with you."

"Well, I won't apologize for sweeping her off her feet," he said with a chuckle.

"And you shouldn't," Katya said, winking. "She will be missed. She's a hard worker and so good with customers."

Cael knew he was grinning like a fool. His elephant was so tickled that his soulmate was being complimented.

He wandered around the store looking at the shelves of glassware and curios, the scratched and dented furniture, and shelves of books.

"Hey," Novi said, joining him at a shelf of old VHS tapes. "I don't think anyone even has a VCR anymore."

"Probably the technology holdouts. My grandma still doesn't know how to change the clock on her oven when the time changes. It drives my mom bonkers when she visits and the clock is wrong."

Novi chuckled and then lifted a small elephant statue. It fit in the palm of her hand, the wooden statue depicting an elephant sitting down, trunk held high and one leg lifted like it was waving.

"That's cool," he said, taking it from her and turning it over in his hands.

"It was in a box I unpacked from an estate. The woman collected elephant statues by the dozens. I've never seen so many of them. I thought this one was really neat so I bought it. For a whopping two dollars."

"Nice," he said. "I know just the place for it."

"Oh?"

"Yep, on the bookshelf I'm going to build for you."

"Aw. Really?"

"Yeah, I mean I've never made one before, but I found a

kit online and it looks pretty easy. I figure I'll get practice putting a bookshelf together and then I'll be prepared for when I get to build a crib."

She beamed at him. "I love it. I'll actually get to keep books now instead of having to read and return them."

He loved that he could do that for her.

"Ready to go, sweetheart?"

"I am. Let me grab my bag."

She hurried to the break room and returned with her bag and the elephant. When they were headed toward her place, she said, "I talked to my mom while we were both on lunch break today and I told her that I was going to move in with you and was packing up after work today."

"Oh? What did she say?"

"She asked if I was aware of how fast we were moving," she said with a light laugh. "And when I told her that I did, but that I also loved you and knew we were meant to be together, she said she was happy for me and would be there to help pack."

"Do you think she's worried about living alone?" he asked.

"I think a little, but she wouldn't tell me if she was. She's kept so much of how she feels about us being on the run close to the vest, even with me. I know she's tired of always moving, always looking over her shoulder, but she's afraid to relax and let down her guard."

"Well, I'm not sure she should relax too much. I mean, we have no idea if your father is still looking for you or not. It would depend on his motivation."

"What do you mean?"

Cael parked in front of the little house and turned off the engine, then faced his mate. "There must be a reason he's kept after you for such a long time. Would even the most dedicated stalker follow you through countless states over two decades? It kind of boggles the mind. So to me it means that he's been told he has to take care of you by a higher-up in his group, most likely his alpha. If it's a direct order, something may hinge on it like a move to a higher rank or something of that nature. He may have no choice but to obey."

"Why couldn't he just say no and leave us alone?"

"You're human, at least mostly, so you don't understand what it means to be under the authority of an alpha. Once we align ourselves to an alpha, it makes it nearly impossible to ignore orders." He touched the side of her neck. "Remember when you bit me the first time we made love?"

She nodded.

"You told me you couldn't help yourself, that you felt like your bear wanted you to mark me so everyone would know that I was mated."

"Right. And?"

"Imagine if you were a full bear. That compulsion you felt to do something your bear wanted to do was too difficult for you to ignore, so double that compulsion in your father and involve his alpha and you've got a recipe for a male who will stop at nothing to get what he wants. Even if he doesn't agree, he might not be willing to risk exile from his group or something worse."

"Worse like what?"

"Death."

"You're saying that maybe his alpha told him to find and kill me or he'd be killed?"

Cael shrugged. "It's all speculation at this point, sweetheart. Even if I could speak to him, I doubt he'd tell me about the inner workings of his shifter group or his motivation for hunting you all these years."

She blew out a breath and looked toward the house. "I want my mom to be safe."

"Then we need to figure out how to get her to the apartment in the park."

"Okay. I hope we can do that sooner rather than later."

"Me too."

They got out of the SUV, and she unlocked the door, calling for her mom as they walked inside. The cozy two-bedroom house smelled like fresh baked bread and seafood.

"In the kitchen, honey," her mom called.

They walked into the kitchen and found her mom ladling soup into bread bowls and setting them on the butcher block table. Novi hugged her and Cael greeted her.

Novi said, "Did you make lobster bisque in bread bowls for us?"

"I did. It's your last night here, I wanted it to be special."

Novi looked at Cael. "It's my favorite meal. We lived in San Francisco for a year and Mom took me to this amazing restaurant for my eleventh birthday, and I got lobster bisque in a sourdough bread bowl. It was amazing. Mom worked on the recipe for years to make it like that place did, and it's my birthday meal now."

"That's neat, I just get a giant bag of Reese's Cups in the mail from my parents," he said. "They're my favorite."

"I'll remember that," Novi said.

He pulled out her chair and they sat, digging into the steaming bowls of thick soup and dunking in torn chunks of the bread bowl. He'd never had anything so good, and when Lori offered him another bowl, he jumped at the chance. While they ate, they talked about Novi moving into his place, which they were careful to refer to as an apartment and not a house, the new job waiting for her in the security office, and her sadness at turning in her notice at the thrift store.

"It's always sad to say goodbye to good bosses," Lori said. "I'm sure you will be missed there. But how exciting to get to work at the park and see the animals every day. And your boyfriend."

Cael nodded. "I'm looking forward to that too."

After they finished the meal, he did the dishes while she and her mom went to pack. He could hear their low voices but couldn't make out what they were saying. When the last dish was dried, he put the towel on the edge of the sink and followed the voices to her bedroom. Novi had him carry her packed things to her car. They spent a few hours packing and talking, and by the time they were all yawning, they'd gotten her packed up.

Novi hugged her mom at the door. "Thank you for being so kind."

"How else would I be?" she asked with a raised brow.

"I don't know, you could give me a hard time about moving in with Cael when we haven't known each other a week."

"I'm not going to tell you how to live your life, honey. I want you to be safe, and it sounds like living at the park is a great place for that to happen. Will I miss you? One hundred percent. Would I try to guilt you into staying here? Absolutely not."

"I heard that one of the apartments is available if you'd like to take it," Cael said.

"Aren't they for employees?"

"Yes, but it's a new complex so they're not taken yet, and my boss said we could offer it to you."

Lori looked suspicious, and then said, "I'll think about it."

Novi nodded, hugged her mom once more, then said, "Come for dinner Friday night."

"Sounds good, honey. I'll be there with bells on."

Novi drove her car, following Cael in the SUV back to the park. He didn't think Lori was going to want to move into the apartment; her "I'll think about it" sounded a lot like "no."

But maybe she'd change her mind and see the value of being in such a protected place. With the security patrols, tall walls, and perimeter videos and alarms, no one got into the park that didn't belong there.

He hoped she'd see what a good idea it was, but in the meantime, he had his sweetheart moving into his place, and that's what mattered. He would do anything to keep Novi safe and with him. She was his everything.

CHAPTER THIRTEEN

Novi adjusted the towels in the apartment bathroom and then turned to the counter, setting a cup with two toothbrushes and a tube of toothpaste on one side of the sink and a hand soap dispenser on the other.

She heard the front door open and flicked off the light. She found Cael balancing a large box under one arm and several grocery sacks hanging from his other arm.

"Need a hand?" she asked.

"Nope, I'm perfectly balanced," he said with a smile, kicking the door shut and heading into the kitchen.

"That's a lot of food," she said.

He put the box on the kitchen table and set the bags on the counter. "Well, we need it to look like we moved in here for one, and for another I thought since we're going to this much trouble to make it look like we're living here that we could stay for the weekend. Like a mini vacation."

"A mini vacation where we still have to go to work," she said.

"Well, yeah," he said, laughing. "But we'll have the complex to ourselves. It'll be nice to sleep with the windows open and get some fresh air, maybe go for a walk after dark and look at the stars."

She went onto her toes and kissed him. "You're so romantic, I love both those ideas."

"Have you heard from your mom?"

"Yep. She texted to say she got home from work and was taking a shower, and then she'd be here. Should be about forty-five minutes, give or take."

He nodded and began to unpack the box.

Novi had only worked a half day at the thrift store, stopped at her mom's place to pick up a few things she'd forgotten to pack, and then spent the afternoon with Cael attempting to make the apartment look lived-in. One of the first things she'd said was that they needed to stock the fridge and cabinets. The apartment—like the others in the complex—was sparsely furnished in the family room, kitchen, and bedroom, but the cabinets in the kitchen and bathroom were empty as was the fridge. She'd brought a set of dishes, cups, and silverware from the thrift store and washed them before setting the table for dinner and organizing the bathroom.

"It's a nice apartment," she said. He'd picked up dinner from the market for them. The special of the day was beef stew with a side of cornbread. She opened the container of stew and inhaled. "Holy crap this smells good."

"Right?" he said. "They make killer cornbread too."

"I can't wait."

"So what were you saying about the apartment?" He straightened from where he'd put away the groceries in the fridge and shut the door.

"That it's nice."

"It is."

"I was just thinking about when my mom moves, that I think we'll be happy here too."

"I'd be happy anywhere as long as you and I are together."

"Me too."

He looked around the kitchen and then down at her. "But I agree about this place. They did a good job designing it, it's really comfortable."

"You sure you won't mind living up here when my mom moves in?"

"I promise. Home is wherever you are, and it really doesn't matter to me if it's here or underground or anywhere else."

She grinned. He said the sweetest things. She was really lucky to have him in her life. They finished putting away the groceries and tidied up, and by the time the stew was bubbling away on the stove and had filled the apartment with its delicious smells, her mom texted to say she'd reached the gate at the back of the park and had accidentally deleted the text with the security code.

Novi texted it to her again and headed out to stand on the walkway and wave her mom up.

"This is nice," her mom said as she walked up the stairs and down the short walkway.

Novi gave her a hug. "It is. Very secure."

Her mom rolled her eyes. "You don't have to keep saying that."

"Well, it's true. The park has high stone walls that are equipped with security cameras and alarms and they have patrols too."

Her mom said nothing, just gave her the old "mom eye."

Novi sighed. "Okay, I won't bring it up again. So long as you're thinking about it."

"I am."

"All right, come and see the inside, it's really cute."

She gave her mom the tour of the two-bedroom apartment and ended in the kitchen, where Cael gave her mom a hug. "Dinner's ready," he said, "I just heated up the cornbread."

"Did you cook all this?" her mom asked as she sat at the small table.

"No, there's a market for the workers that sells full meals to take home. You know I love a good beef stew."

"Me too."

Cael ladled stew into their bowls, and Novi served up wedges of cornbread and butter. The trio ate in silence for a little while. Novi thought it was the best stew she'd ever had in her life.

"Well, if this is the sort of food you have access to at the park, I'd say you picked a great place," her mom said, putting her spoon in the empty bowl. "It's delicious."

They took a plate of cookies and drinks into the family room and talked about work and the park. An hour later, her mom was yawning and saying it was time to head home before it got too late.

She walked her mom to the door and gave her a hug. "I'm so glad you could come visit."

"Me too. We can make it a weekly thing if you'd like, take turns having a meal here and at my place."

Novi tried not to let her disappointment show. "Sounds good. Drive safe and text me when you're home."

"I'll do that."

Novi opened the door and let her mom out.

"I'll walk you down," Cael said, hurrying after her.

"Oh, I'll come," Novi said.

"Nah," Cael said, giving her a wink. "I'll be right back."

He pulled the door shut so fast that Novi's hair fluffed up around her shoulders with the breeze. She stared at the door for a long moment and then she smiled. Her mate wanted a few minutes alone with her mom.

She wondered what he was going to talk to her about.

~

Cael walked Lori down the steps and toward her car, which was parked in one of the lined spaces in front of the complex. "Thank you for dinner," Lori said.

"It was my pleasure. You're welcome anytime."

Lori unlocked her door, dropped her bag on the seat, and then turned to look at him. "I think you want to talk to me about something?"

"Very much so." Cael rocked back on his heels, his nerves kicking up. He cleared his throat and said, "I'd like to ask for your blessing. I want to ask Novi to marry me."

Lori said nothing for a long moment, and Cael wondered if she would say no.

"I like you. I think you're good for Novi, and it's hard for me to trust anyone. I've spent her whole life trying to keep her safe, and that's always meant just the two of us, not letting anyone else get too close. I've always been afraid that Keir would find us somehow, that he might be searching for our names online or using private investigators to dig us up. It's been incredibly hard and stressful all these years." She said nothing for a minute, then said, "But you make her happy. I can tell she feels free to be with you, feels safe. I'm so happy for her, for both of you. So yes, you have my permission."

Cael's elephant wanted to trumpet in triumph, but he managed to keep a lid on his exuberance. Grinning, he hugged Lori. "Thank you so much!"

Lori chuckled and patted his back. "Of course. Welcome to the family. Do you know when you're going to ask?"

"Tomorrow night. I wanted it to be a week from the day we met."

Lori's eyes went luminous for a moment and then she cleared her throat. "You'll keep her safe?"

"On my life. Once she's finished working at the thrift store, she won't have to travel back and forth to her job. The park is truly safe. I think it's the safest place for you both."

"I know you do. I'm just not ready for that kind of move. It feels too permanent."

Cael frowned. "What do you mean?"

"Obviously, Novi is planning to live with you forever. You've got a job and friends here, she's going to be working at the park too. That's settling down roots. I'm...honestly afraid to do that."

He nodded as understanding filled him. "You think if you settled down, you'll be inviting him to come find you. And Novi."

"Well, she has you and you're clearly the sort of guy who can take care of her. But I've always felt safer being able to pick up and go at a moment's notice."

"Maybe you don't have to run anymore. You're family to me now, Lori. I want you to be safe and happy, and I think you could have that here."

"We'll see."

She said goodnight and got into her car. He watched her back away and head toward the gate. In the distance, he could hear the gate creak as it opened and then closed. He sighed. She was stubborn and full of fear. He appreciated how difficult her life had been trying to keep Novi safe, but he was one hundred percent positive that they were safe in the park. Novi deserved to live a real life and to stay in one place with people who loved her and wanted good things for her.

And Lori deserved that too.

He hoped she'd get it, that she'd see the complex as a good and safe place to stay and start her life over. It was time for her to live her life too.

CHAPTER FOURTEEN

Keir sat on the couch that faced the front door in the tiny house that the human Lori called home. His males were scattered around the room, two standing at the front door. When he'd arrived an hour ago, they'd just missed her, apparently. Her car was gone, but a sweep of the house had told him she'd come home and taken a shower and changed. It appeared that the daughter was no longer living there, which was a complication he hadn't expected, but it didn't matter at any rate. His plan was to take Lori captive, lure Novi inside, and then take them both somewhere remote and kill them.

So they settled in to wait.

The minutes crept by, and his annoyance grew. He fidgeted until he couldn't sit anymore and took to pacing from one side of the small room to the other.

"Where the fuck is she?" he demanded harshly, his voice just loud enough for his males to hear. She'd been gone for hours.

As if on cue, a car swung into the driveway, the headlights seeping around the edges of the plastic miniblinds. His bear snarled, happy to finally have the source of their problems within reach.

He would snuff out her life, and her daughter's life, and move the hell on with his own.

The headlights stayed on, the engine idling.

"What's going on?" he asked.

One of the males at the window carefully peeked between the slats. "She's just sitting there. She's staring at the house, but she's not moving."

Keir knew they couldn't just charge out of the house and grab her from her car—she could simply drive off when she saw him. They had to wait for her to get into the house and then they could subdue her.

The lights swung away from the house and the tires squealed as the car revved and quickly disappeared. Keir raced to the window and ripped the blinds aside in time to see the red taillights turn the corner and disappear.

"Fuck!" he roared.

She must have felt his presence in some way, realized that danger was waiting inside. Humans did have an ancient fight-or-flight response when it came to shifters, they just didn't know the reason they were afraid of some people was because they were also animals. He wondered if that was why she was able to elude him all these years, always be one step ahead of him. She was somehow tuned into him and knew when to run.

It was infuriating.

He needed to end her hold over him and soon.

"What now?" Donovan asked.

"We wait."

~

Novi's phone rang just as she'd tugged off Cael's shirt. It was tempting to ignore the call, but she didn't give her number out to too many people.

She kissed Cael's pec and wiggled her brows at him as she reached for her phone on the nightstand.

Her mom's name was on the screen. "Hey Mom," she said.

Cael sat next to her on the bed.

"Novi!" her mom's voice was panicked.

She lurched to her feet. "Mom? What's wrong?"

"I don't know," she said, breathing hard. "I pulled into the driveway and I thought...it felt like someone was watching me."

"Are you still at home?"

"No, I left right away. I didn't even get out of the car."

She turned to look at Cael who was now on his phone. He whispered, "Tell her to come here," and Novi nodded.

"Come back to the park, Mom. You can stay in the apartment next to ours."

"Are you sure?"

"Yes, Mom! Of course."

"Ask if she's being followed," Cael said.

Novi relayed his words to her mom.

"I don't think so. I didn't see any cars in the driveway or on the street, but it was just this terrible feeling. Like something awful was waiting for me in the house. I haven't felt like that since..." Her voice dropped off.

Novi finished her sentence, "Since he tried to run you off the road a few years ago?"

"Yes." Her mom's voice was high and strained.

"Aw Mom, I'm so sorry. I'm really glad that you trusted your instincts and left. How far away are you?"

"Um, ten minutes."

"Sure you're not being followed?"

"Pretty sure. It's late, so there aren't a lot of cars out."

"Okay, good."

She looked at Cael, and he said, "Tell her that I'll be waiting at the gate to escort her here along with a few of the guards."

She relayed his message.

"Okay, honey, thank you. I'm really sorry about all this."

"What are you sorry about?" Novi asked.

"Because you begged me to stay there, but I was too stubborn and now I might be bringing danger there."

"If no one is following you then you're not bringing danger anywhere, Mom."

"He found me. I don't know how but he did."

Novi wanted to argue that it could've been something else triggering her worry, but she knew in her heart that her mom had a kind of sixth sense about that sort of thing and if she thought it was Keir, then it was.

"It'll be okay, I promise. The park is so safe."

Cael kissed Novi's cheek. "Alistair is meeting me with some other guards at the gate. Tell her we'll see her soon."

Novi nodded, relayed his last message and said, "Stay on the phone with me until you see Cael at the gate."

"Okay."

There was an awkward pause, and Novi didn't know what to say. She wanted to alleviate the tension, so she said, "What did you and Cael talk about when he walked you to your car?"

"I'm not telling," she said, with a chuckle.

"Boo. Fine, fine, keep secrets from your only daughter."

"It's nothing bad, I'll just say that. And he did ask me about staying in the apartment. I should've listened."

"We all make mistakes, don't let it get to you, okay?"

"I see some guys at the gate."

"Good. I'll see you in a few."

The call ended and Novi sat down on the bed. She let out

115

a trembling breath, grateful her mom had made it to the park safely. Then she realized she wasn't wearing her shirt, so she picked it up from the bed and put it on. She found her shoes in the family room and hurried to the door. She stood out on the walkway, listening for the vehicles. A few minutes later, her mom's car parked in front of the complex, and Cael got out of one of the park's marked SUVs.

Novi waved at her mom as she got out of her car.

"Welcome back," Novi said.

"Thanks, honey."

Cael spoke to whoever was driving the SUV for a few moments, and then joined Novi and her mom on the walkway.

"Here's your key," Cael said, handing her mom a keyring with a single key hanging from it. "I think it would be a good idea if you took a couple days off work and stayed here. Some of the park guards are going to head to your house and look around, so we'll need your keys."

"I don't want anyone to get hurt," her mom said, squeezing her car keys in her hand.

"No one will, I promise. They're very good at what they do."

She nodded and handed him the keys.

"Let's go look in your new place, Mom," Novi said. She looked at Cael and said, "She could use some supplies for the night."

"On it, love." He pecked her cheek and whispered, "I'm going to your mom's place. I'll text you when I know what's up. In the meantime, I'll send one of the females with supplies for your mom."

"Thank you, be careful."

"I will."

They both said they loved each other, and she watched him stride swiftly away and down the walkway.

"He'll be fine," Novi said, smiling at her mom.

"Who are you telling? Me or yourself?" she asked with a smirk.

Novi chuckled. "How about both of us?"

"He's not going alone, right?"

"No."

"Good. I don't trust your father. He's dangerous."

"I know, but Cael's strong. He'll be fine. Now let's check out your apartment."

Her mom unlocked the door next to her and Cael's apartment, and they walked in to find an identical one. It was done up in shades of blue from a navy couch to a light blue comforter.

Her mom sat on the couch and sighed deeply. "I appreciate this. It feels weird."

"What does?" Novi asked as she joined her on the couch.

"You taking care of me for a change."

"I learned from the best."

CHAPTER FIFTEEN

Cael didn't have the greatest sense of smell. Some of the other shifters, like the wolves, had incredible senses, but elephants weren't known for that. He could smell better than a human, but at the moment he couldn't smell anything inside Lori and Novi's house save for the two females.

But he could definitely tell that someone had been in the house because the backdoor lock was busted, and while nothing really seemed out of place, there was an air of "not quite right" that he couldn't put his finger on.

Alistair put his hands on his hips and looked around. "I'd say more than one was here."

Jupiter said, "I'm picking up four or five different males, all bears."

Nathan, one of the gorillas, nodded. "I'm getting that as well. It doesn't look like they did anything but break in and wait. Lori's lucky she didn't come in."

Cael agreed. "I wonder how he found her."

"He's obviously a very determined male," Alistair said. "He's been tracking her for two decades and, according to Lori, he's come close a number of times. He's probably using some kind of database search to check for her and Novi's information, like background checks for jobs or the houses they rent."

"Novi said they don't even use credit cards, they buy the prepaid ones, but their whole lives are cash. They're really careful."

"However he found them, we need to keep them both safe. Lori's okay with moving into the complex?" Jupiter asked.

"For now, yes. She's mostly just freaked out, so I don't think she's had a chance to think much past tonight."

"We'll arrange escorts for her to and from her job," Jupiter said. "I put out a call to Joss, and there are plenty of wolves and lions willing to help out."

"I'm going to pack a bag for her," Cael said. He'd gotten a list of things from Novi that her mom requested, so he didn't have to guess what she might need. Nathan offered to pack up the bathroom necessities, and Cael left him to that, heading to the bedroom to collect her clothes and shoes.

Alistair leaned against the doorjamb. "I fixed the door so it's locked now and can't be opened again, but if they want in badly enough, they'll get in. She can call the landlord and have them replace the lock tomorrow."

"Thanks." Cael grabbed handfuls of socks and undergarments from the dresser and stuffed them into a suitcase from the closet, then turned to face the hanging clothes. "I wish they didn't have to deal with this."

"Me too. I hope he will give up and leave them alone, but I think he's determined to get to them, so we'll need to be on our toes."

"I'll drive Novi back and forth to work. She only has a little over a week left."

"She can't just quit?"

"She doesn't want to leave her boss in the lurch. It's too bad we can't get Lori a job in the park."

"Not as long as she's oblivious to shifters. There's too much of a chance for her to overhear something she shouldn't."

When he was finished packing, he carried the suitcase out to the unmarked SUV and got behind the wheel. He waited for Alistair, Jupiter, and Nathan to come out. Nathan set the bag of toiletries in the backseat and joined Jupiter in the other SUV. Alistair joined Cael. Cael put the SUV into gear and backed away from the house.

"You look disappointed," Alistair said.

"I kind of wish that Keir had been there."

"What would you have done if he had?"

"Make sure he knows that Novi and Lori are under our protection."

"He doesn't seem to be the sort of male to take a hint or give up easily, so I don't think speaking to him would change anything."

"I know." Keir was strong-willed and that meant he would need to be physically dealt with. Cael had never gone on the offense like that before, but he knew what Alistair was getting at. If Keir and his people had been at the apartment there would've been a battle and lives could've been lost. He didn't want any of his friends getting hurt by this jackass, but if push came to shove, his people would stand with him. Novi was his mate and that made her family to the memory as well as the other shifter groups. They always protected the mates and children, no matter what.

He glanced in the rearview mirror to make sure no one was following them, and the street behind him was empty. He wouldn't relax until they made it back to the park, taking a few back roads and side streets to backtrack and ensure they weren't being tailed by Keir and his people. Once he was with his beautiful soulmate again and they could lock the door and put the worries of the night behind them, then he'd relax.

But as a shifter male with a mate to protect, he knew he'd never really relax. He'd always be worried for her safety, until the threat against her and her mother was put down for good. If Keir was smart, he'd realize that Lori and Novi were off-limits to him for good and take a hike.

And if he didn't, then Cael would be ready to fight for his mate and her mom.

They were his family now, and Novi was the center of his world. Her safety was paramount, and no male with a twenty-year grudge would take her from him.

That much he knew for sure.

Cael shook out his ears and stretched in the paddock. The afternoon sun was warm on his skin, and he was really looking forward to just hanging out and relaxing, but it was Saturday and there were VIP tours happening, so he couldn't just find a shady corner and doze off. With Novi.

He very much wanted to do that. He loved when she climbed on him and stretched out, or curled up over his front legs and rested on him. She felt safe with him in both forms and that meant the world to him.

It had been almost three weeks since Keir had broken into the house, and they hadn't seen hide nor hair of him. While they weren't taking it easy with the safety of the park and Novi and Lori, he wondered if the male had taken a hint and left for good. Novi and Lori didn't think that was likely, but he thought the male was most likely watching the house and had seen them come and look around.

Lori had settled into the routine of getting driven to and

from her job, but Cael could see how much it rankled her to not be able to just take off if she felt threatened. Novi said it was because they'd been on the run for so long that Lori didn't know how to relax. He supposed if he'd been hunted by a bear shifter for two decades that he'd be paranoid too.

Novi was working in the security office making the photo albums, which she adored doing. Not only did she get to see all the pictures from the tours which she enjoyed looking at, but she was also tasked with ensuring that there were no issues with the photos that might lead to someone suspecting the animals weren't quite right.

Like when his elephant had odd-colored eyes.

"Hey handsome," Novi said as she walked toward him wearing a beige uniform. A metal bucket swung from one hand, a few red apples peeking over the rim.

He gave a low trumpet of happiness which made her smile.

"Mom can't believe that you guys let me in here. She was very jealous." Novi lifted an apple, and he took it from her with his trunk and ate it. She gave him a second one, and then he followed her as she made her way to the three others in the paddock and gave them all apples. He heard a Jeep coming and gave her a nudge with his trunk and gestured away from the fence. They never wanted the people posing as animal handlers to be a distraction for the VIPs.

Novi finished giving the apples to Kelley, Alistair, and Indio, and then walked with him away from the fence.

She sat behind some brush at the pond's edge and hugged her arms around her knees. He stood next to her, keeping one eye on the Jeep to see if Indio or Alistair might have found their soulmate.

"Rhapsody wants to have a girl's night tonight, just her and me. Kelley's going to watch Khap for her."

He nodded at her when she looked up at him. He was so

glad she and Rhapsody were becoming friends. For Novi, it was the first time in her life that she'd actually been able to make a real friend that she could keep. She'd had friends in the past, but because of her father, they'd often had to leave without saying goodbye and not keep in touch with anyone, for fear Keir could find out where they were through their acquaintances.

Now she didn't have to worry. She was protected by him and surrounded by people who wanted her to be happy and safe.

The Jeep moved on and Novi sighed. "I don't want to go back to work, I love hanging out here with you."

She'd come to sit with him on break, and he was always thrilled for the time with her when he was in his shift.

He made a noise of agreement.

"You'll come find me in the office?"

He offered her his trunk, and she helped herself up with it. He nodded and she smiled at him.

"I'll miss you."

She picked up the bucket, and he followed her to the shed. He could hear a Jeep rumbling near, and she hurried into the shed and waved at him before closing the door so that the VIP didn't see her leave the paddock.

"Love you," she called through the door.

He gave a happy rumble and listened to her open the door in the floor and then shut it again. She'd head back to the security office to make the albums for the day's VIPs.

The afternoon dragged, and he was going crazy without his sweetheart, but Alistair insisted that even mated males had to spend time in the paddocks for the tours, so he grudgingly agreed.

When the last tour had left the area, they waited for the patrol to come by and let them know it was safe to shift back, which took anywhere from twenty minutes to an hour, depending on how quick the tour finished up and the humans were all gone from the area. He hurried to the shed and shifted as soon as he was inside, relief flooding him at being able to see Novi soon.

He was tugging on his jeans when Kelley came inside and shifted. "I take it you're excited to go see Novi?"

"You know it. Isn't it hard for you to be away from Rhapsody?"

"Absolutely, but it would look weird if she posed as a handler and had Khap in a carrier on her back. It's just safer for them to be home and away from the public eye."

"Good point. I heard you're on kid-duty while the girls hang out. Want some company?"

"That would be great. We can watch a movie."

"Sounds good."

Cael said goodbye and hurried down the stairs, making his way back up to the employee cafeteria. He crossed the park to the security office and saw through the windows that Novi was handing a photo album to a young woman. He waited outside until they were finished. Novi opened the door for the woman and said, "Enjoy the park!"

"Thank you for the album, it's so cute."

Novi waved at the woman as she walked away and then smiled at Cael. "That was the last book. I'm hungry for ice cream."

"I thought you were eating in the market with Rhapsody?"

"We are, but that's not for two more hours. I'm ready for a treat."

"Sounds good to me."

"See ya later, Javan," she called into the office.

"Have a good night, Novi," Javan called back.

She stepped into Cael's arms and gave him a hug. "Missed you," he said.

"I missed you too."

They walked toward the ice cream stand that was run by Tayme and his mate, Rory. He took Novi's hand and told her he was going to hang out with Kelley and Khap while she and Rhapsody had their girls' night.

"That sounds fun. He's such a cutie."

"He is."

"I can't wait to have a baby. But I'd like to get married first."

"Absolutely. My parents will want to come out for the wedding, even if we do something small."

"I've always wanted a fall wedding, when the leaves are so pretty."

"That sounds perfect. I guess I better come up with a romantic proposal."

She stopped walking and he thought she was going to say something teasing to him, but when he looked at her, she was staring over her shoulder.

"What's wrong?" he asked.

"That's...my mom."

He looked in the direction she was, and his brows went up. Lori was seated at a picnic table with a burger and fries basket in front of her. Across from her was the gorilla alpha Atticus, who also had a burger and fries basket, but his basket had two burgers in it instead of just one. They were smiling and talking in between bites.

"Wow," he said.

"Who is that?" Novi asked.

"Atticus."

She turned to look at Cael with a questioning look and he mouthed "gorilla."

"Ah. I knew the name sounded familiar. I wonder when that happened."

"She didn't say anything to you about meeting him?"

"No, but I haven't talked to her since dinner last night." Novi glanced once more at her mom and then smiled at Cael. "My mom made a friend."

"It seems so."

They continued on their walk to the ice cream stand. "Do you think they might be soulmates?"

"It's possible. But like you said, they could just be friends having dinner."

"Either way, I'm really happy for her. She deserves to have a friend other than me. I'm certainly much happier with you in my life."

"Aw," he said, "I'm much happier too."

They stopped at the ice cream stand and got in line.

"I think," she said, "that my favorite thing about the park is the tour where we met. But the ice cream stand is a close second."

"Me too. My life changed for the better that day."

"Mine too."

They got ice cream cones and walked around the park, enjoying their time together before they parted for a few hours to spend time with their friends. He couldn't believe how much had changed for him since she'd come into his life, but he'd never been happier. Soon he'd ask her to marry him, and they'd have a fall wedding like she wanted. And then they'd have a baby, and hopefully more than one, to fill up their home with love and laughter.

He was feeling damn sentimental as he kissed her goodbye and went to hang out with Kelley and Khap.

Novi was the most amazing female he'd ever met, and that she loved him and wanted to spend the rest of her life with him made him thank his lucky stars for the day the VIP tour coupon showed up in her mailbox addressed to someone else.

That little mix-up had brought them together, and he was a better male for having her in his life.

Whatever the future brought their way, he knew they could handle it together.

The End

COMING MAY 2021 IN THE SABLE
COVE SERIES

Must Love Mermen

www.rebutlerauthor.com

CONTACT THE AUTHOR

Website: http://www.rebutlerauthor.com

Email: rebutlerauthor@gmail.com

Facebook: www.facebook.com/R.E.ButlerAuthorPage

Every Sunset Forever

Every Blissful Moment

Every Heavenly Moment

Every Miraculous Moment

Every Angelic Moment

The Necklace Chronicles

The Tribe's Bride

The Gigolo's Bride

The Tiger's Bride

The Alpha Wolf's Mate

The Jaguar's Bride

The Author's True Mate

Norlanian Brides

Paoli's Bride

Warrick's Bride

Dex's Bride

Norlanian Brides Volume One

Villi's Bride

Dero's Bride

Saber Chronicles

Saber Chronicles Volume One (Books One - Four)

Sable Cove

Must Love Familiars

Must Love Mermen (Coming Soon)

Tails

Memory

Atticus (Coming Soon)

Wiccan-Were-Bear

A Curve of Claw

A Flash of Fang

A Price for a Princess

A Bond of Brothers

A Bead of Blood

A Twitch of Tail

A Promise on White Wings

A Slash of Savagery

Awaken a Wolf

Daeton's Journey

A Dragon for December

A Muse for Mishka

A Wish for Their Woman

The Wiccan-Were-Bear Series Volume One

The Wiccan-Were-Bear Series Volume Two

The Wiccan-Were-Bear Series Volume Three

Wilde Creek

Volume One (Books 1 and 2)

Volume Two (Books 3 and 4)

Volume Three (Books 5 and 6)

Volume Four (Books 7 and 8)

The Wolf's Mate

The Wolf's Mate Book 1: Jason & Cadence

The Wolf's Mate Book 2: Linus & The Angel

The Wolf's Mate Book 3: Callie & The Cats

~

Coming Soon in the Sable Cove Series: Must Love Mermen

- Lonely merman hero? Check
- Fairy heroine floundering at sea? Check
- Mysterious magic? Double check

After being exiled from his merfolk tribe two years earlier, all Merman Cassian wants to do is live out his life in the quiet seaside town of Sable Cove. Taking over for the lighthouse keeper and watching the shores for trouble keep him plenty busy and helps keep his mind off how lonely he is. When a beautiful fairy's boat drifts into the cove, Cassian knows she's his siren—the one female on the planet meant for him.

Nature fairy Ziarena is thankful to be rescued by the sexiest merman she's ever met in her life, especially when she realizes he's her true mate. When Cassian and Zia travel to her home, their boat is attacked by merpeople who abduct Zia. The danger they face is enough to bring something magical to life within Zia, but no one knows how it's possible. Can they figure out what Zia is or will it remain a mystery forever?

~